CHESAPEAKE CRIMES

HOMICIDAL HOLIDAYS

IN THE SAME SERIES

Chesapeake Crimes
Chesapeake Crimes 2
Chesapeake Crimes 3
Chesapeake Crimes: They Had It Comin'
Chesapeake Crimes: This Job is Murder

CHESAPEAKE CRIMES

HOMICIDAL HOLIDAYS

Fourteen Tales of Murder and Merriment

Edited by Donna Andrews,
Barb Goffman, and Marcia Talley

Introduction by Rhys Bowen

WILDSIDE PRESS

Chesapeake Crimes: Homicidal Holidays

Coordinating Editors
Donna Andrews
Barb Goffman
Marcia Talley

Editorial Panel
Christina Freeburn
John Gilstrap
Alan Orloff

This edition is published in 2014 by Wildside Press, LLC.
www.wildsidebooks.com

Contents

CHRISTMAS

INTRODUCTION

One thing I've learned during a long career as a writer is that a good short story is one of the hardest things to write. To capture mood, character, tension, and a satisfying climax in a few pages requires more skill than having the luxury of a novel to get things right. That's why I'm so impressed that the writers of Chesapeake Crimes seem to deliver quality work in anthology after anthology.

This one is especially fun as the theme is holidays. And who hasn't wanted to commit a murder at a family holiday celebration?

Not surprisingly the favorite holiday for this anthology is Halloween, followed closely by Christmas. But if you're expecting traditional pudding or trick and treat, you're in for a pleasant surprise. So many of these stories come with new approaches to the holiday theme, like Clyde Linsley's wickedly clever "Sauce for the Goose," or Carla Coupe's masterful twists in "Shadow Boxer."

Some are pure fun like Barb Goffman's opening story for Groundhog Day and Donna Andrews's zany Christmas story involving her beloved heroine Meg Langslow and her impossible family. The mood can also be unsettling as in Art Taylor's "Premonition" and Timothy Bentler-Jungr's poignant "Last Rites." And let's not forget less well known holidays like Talk Like a Pirate Day and Cathy Wiley's "Dead Men Tell No Tales."

Have fun with this whole year of holiday stories. I certainly did!

—Rhys Bowen

GROUNDHOG DAY

THE SHADOW KNOWS

by Barb Goffman

"Good Lord, Gus, what's got you so down on this beautiful Saturday morning?"

I nearly spit out my coffee onto the diner's Formica counter. "Beautiful? Says who?"

Sally pointed to the picture window by the front booths. Another foot of snow had fallen overnight, weighing down the tree limbs and power lines. I'd almost frozen solid as I cleared my driveway an hour before. Nothing good about any of that.

"Don't tell me you can't appreciate the splendor out there, Gus," Sally said as she grabbed the pot off the coffee maker behind the counter and refilled my chipped mug. "The way the snow is sparkling in the sunlight. It's so bright and fresh. Makes you glad to be alive."

Hmph. "You maybe." I reached for the pepper to spice up my scrambled eggs, and I knocked over the salt. Darn it. I quickly threw a pinch of salt over my left shoulder to ward off bad luck.

The bell over the front door jangled as my pal Bobby came in, stamping the snow off his boots. "Good morning, everyone. Happy Groundhog Day!"

The rest of the customers nodded and returned Bobby's greetings, and Sally smiled at him as he took the stool next to mine. Why was everyone always so doggone cheerful on this blasted day?

"Usual?" she asked as Bobby unzipped his jacket.

"Yes, ma'am." He clapped my back and grinned at me. "Happy Groundhog Day, Gus."

I glared his way. Bobby loved needling me. He knew how I felt about Groundhog Day and especially our resident groundhog, Missisquoi Moe. That damn woodchuck was surely in cahoots with the devil, causing our town to suffer through horrible winters every year.

"Moe saw his shadow this morning. Six more weeks of winter," Bobby sing-songed.

"Yeah, I heard." I cursed under my breath. "I had been hoping for an early spring, for once."

Most groundhogs don't actually control the weather, but here in Missisquoi, ours were different. When I was a kid, every few years we had an early spring. Not anymore. We got our first town groundhog forty-plus years ago and practically every darn year since, he'd predicted a long winter. The prediction always came true. Always. That's how I knew our groundhogs had special powers. If our town selectmen were pulling the strings like in other places, the predictions would have been wrong at least some of the time. But Moe and his ancestors were dead on year after year after year.

Spooky, if you ask me.

Sally set Bobby's pancakes with extra maple syrup down in front of him. "Is that what's bothering you, Gus?" She pushed a lock of her wavy gray hair back into her bun. "What did you expect? This is northern Vermont, for heaven's sake."

I swallowed a bite of bacon. "I expect Moe to get with the program. The news keeps talking about that global warming. Well, it's high time a bit of that warming came here, don't you think?"

Bobby laughed. "Maybe you should pay Moe a visit and discuss it with him. I'm sure it would make all the difference." He winked at Sally, and then she chuckled, too.

I sipped my coffee, thinking. Bobby was right. If I wanted our weather to change, I needed to do something to make it happen. Sitting on my rump hadn't been working. And I needed to do it soon, before Moe met some female groundhog and starting adding little ones to the ancient family line.

Yep. I should have thought of it before. I needed to get rid of that groundhog.

* * * *

In late May the last of the year's snow finally melted—darn groundhog—and I was ready to put my plan into action. I'd spent the previous few months studying the big wildlife sanctuary a few miles from my house where Moe lived. I cased the joint, tracking the pesky rodent's schedule and plotting the best way to get at him unobserved.

The sanctuary kept Moe in an enormous chain-link pen on the edge of the woods. Bushes, branches, and scatterings of hay covered the ground inside. During the spring and summer, Moe was active most days in the mid-morning and late afternoon, scurrying about. But in the early afternoon, he spent his time sleeping in his burrow or lying in the hay, soaking up the sun. That, I decided, was the time to grab him. His cage's gate had a latch that I could easily open. I just had to wait until no one else was around.

Easy peasy.

I should never have thought that, of course. Never tempt fate. Every time I went to the sanctuary, animal keepers or nature lovers or both were milling about. I'd hang by Moe's cage, watching, waiting for my moment. Time and time again, the coast would appear clear, but just as I prepared to dash in and grab the critter, someone would come by. I had so many close calls, it was a miracle I hadn't developed an ulcer. I couldn't linger near the damn pen all the time, of course, or people would grow suspicious, so I wasted a lot of my days off wandering around the whole sanctuary, pretending to be interested in all the animals.

When August loomed, I realized I needed to revise my plan. When would no one be there? On a rainy day. But not just any rainy day. Some granola types might enjoy hiking around in a light rain. I had to wait for a real downpour. As if the devil was trying to stop me, a drought set in about then. But I wouldn't give up. I bought a rabbit's foot for good luck and waited. It had to rain eventually.

And it did. The morning of my birthday, August 22nd, I awoke to thunder and lightning. Wind whipped against the clapboard siding, and sheets of rain sluiced down the windows of my house. Yes! I called in sick, then drove to a grocery store outside of town where no one knew me. I bought bread, lunchmeats, and corn chips for myself and a couple of apples, a few carrots, and a head of lettuce for Moe. I didn't normally keep that healthy stuff in the house, but I'd read that groundhogs like 'em. I headed home and sliced up the apples and carrots and ripped the lettuce into small pieces. I put the food in plastic bags and tucked them inside a knapsack. Then I went to the closet, removed the eighteen-inch cage I'd ordered months before from some outfit on Amazon, and stowed it in my truck. All ready to go, except it wasn't time yet. Back in the house I went, spending hours flipping through TV channels, waiting for early afternoon to come, when Moe would be most vulnerable. Finally after lunch, when I could barely stand to wait another minute, I pulled on my boots, shouldered my knapsack, and slipped a rubbery blue rain poncho over my head. I felt calm as I drove toward the sanctuary, knowing that victory soon would be mine.

I parked my truck behind a large berm at the edge of the woods, about fifty yards from the sanctuary entrance. No one would spot it there. Then I flipped the poncho's hood over my head, tucked the cage under my arm, and started sloshing through the muddy woods, keeping the trail to Moe's pen in sight.

The walk had never seemed so long before. The rain kept pounding me, and the wind was ripping leaves off the trees, sending them sailing right at my face, kamikaze style. I shook my head and blinked repeatedly. Not only was water cascading off the poncho, it was dripping from my eyelashes and nose. I kept marching, all the while trying to shake the water off, just like a dog.

Suddenly my boot smacked hard against something, and I began to flail. As I pitched forward, the cage flew from my hands. I hit the ground hard, my right knee and wrist bearing the brunt of the fall. *Son of a bitch. That hurt.* I lay there for a minute in the soggy leaves, trying to catch my breath and cursing the groundhog while the rain continued to pour. For a second I thought about quitting, but no, I wasn't going to give up. Instead I took a deep breath, shakily stood, and continued on my quest.

I found the cage a few yards away. Its door was busted. *Gosh darn it.* Now I'd have to catch the groundhog with my bare hands. I kicked the cage and nearly screamed from the pain that shot through my big toe. I leaned over, hands on my knees, panting hard.

When I got a hold of that groundhog, I'd wring its furry neck.

After a minute or two, I headed off again, limping. When I finally neared Moe's pen, I was soaked to the skin, and had half a mind to send a nasty letter to the poncho company. But first things first. I paused and peered around. The area was deserted. Thank God. I hobbled over to the cage, lifted the latch, and shuffled inside. That's when I spotted another flaw in my plan. On sunny days, Moe liked to lie out on the hay, which would have made him easy to catch, but now, I couldn't spot him at all.

"Here, Moe," I called.

No response. That bastard rodent was hiding from me.

I started limping around the enclosure, rustling the shrubs and hay, trying to flush Moe out. At the entrance to his burrow, I laid out the apple and carrot slices like a trail, hoping they'd entice him if he was in there. Then I stood out of sight and waited.

And waited and waited. Any second now, someone from the sanctuary could be coming by, and my plan would be ruined. *C'mon, you rat bastard. Come out.* I hunched down behind a bush, hoping it would work as camouflage, but after a few minutes, I had to stand up. My right knee ached too much to crouch like that for long.

So I began pacing. Why wasn't Moe taking the bait? I stared at the burrow, sending mental messages to Moe, willing him to come out, when suddenly—oh, crap, now of all times—I had to pee. *Had to.* I hurried over to a corner of the enclosure, unzipped my jeans, and began to relieve myself.

That was the moment, of course, when Moe crept from his burrow and began eating the carrots. *Son of a bitch.* Normally I could stop midstream, but not today. So I stood there, helpless, while my body did its thing and Moe ate and the rain continued to come down as if a dam had broken. The seconds felt like hours. Finally I finished, zipped up, and dashed for Moe, but he saw me coming, natch, and scurried off. Afraid he'd scamper into his burrow again, I yanked off my useless poncho and stuffed it in the opening. Then I chased Moe around his cage for a good three minutes. I came close to catching him a few times, but he always eluded me, with—I could swear—a glint in his eye.

Ultimately, in an act of desperation, I threw myself at him, like a football player making a tackle. Mud and hay flew up, practically blinding me, while Moe thrashed beneath me, desperate to escape. I grabbed his coarse brown fur and wrenched him to my chest. I'd got him!

The smile that began to creep across my face was instantly erased when a whistle so deafening it could have awakened the dead erupted from that animal. Clutching Moe tight, I held him at arm's length hoping to save my hearing should he decide to scream again. That was when he started kicking. I tried to hold him off, but soon he connected, scratching my cheek, drawing blood. Damn, his feet had sharp claws.

Instinctively, I touched my hand to my cheek, and the beast bit me! Dear God, I thought he'd taken a chunk out of my neck. I would have punched him, but that would have given him the chance to escape. Instead I stumbled over to my knapsack and stuffed him in. I zipped it up almost all the way, leaving just an inch or so open so he could breathe. I stopped a second, catching my own breath, and surveyed the pen. Hay and pieces of carrots, lettuce, and apples were strewn all about. Clear signs that a struggle had occurred. I shook my head. This had all seemed so simple when I'd planned it.

Then Moe began to screech again. How could such a loud sound come out of such a small animal? Begging him to shut up, I slipped the knapsack on, arranging the pack over my chest so I could be sure Moe wouldn't jump out. Then I grabbed my poncho, limped out of the pen, wiped my fingerprints off the latch, and headed back to the woods, my toe throbbing and knee aching with every step.

Finally, after the longest, wettest walk of my life, I made it back to my truck. I tossed the knapsack and poncho onto the passenger seat, threw the truck into gear, and hightailed it out of there. I was so wet and cold and pissed off that I had to fight the urge to floor the accelerator. Moe kept squirming inside my knapsack, hissing, making the bag jump, as if it were possessed. I felt stupid doing it, but I leaned over, found the end of the seatbelt, and strapped the bag in. Then I turned on the radio loud to drown Moe out. Blue Oyster Cult's "Don't Fear the Reaper" was playing. Perfect. I wasn't planning to kill Moe. That surely would bring bad luck. But I didn't mind putting the fear of God in him.

I headed out to the far side of the county, down quiet country roads, over two covered bridges, passing faded barns and houses even older than the century-old one I lived in. I intended to dump Moe in some isolated field far enough away from the sanctuary that he couldn't find his way back. I didn't know if groundhogs had a homing instinct, like pigeons, but I wasn't taking any chances.

After driving for half an hour, I figured I'd gone far enough. I pulled over to the side of the road, turned down the radio, and grabbed the knapsack. In the sudden quiet, the *thwack thwack thwack* of the windshield wipers seemed awful loud. I set the pack against the steering wheel, aiming to open it far enough from my face so the bugger wouldn't be able to get another swipe at me. I unzipped the bag tentatively. My face still stung from the last time he got at me.

To my surprise, Moe didn't try to jump out. He was wiggling, so I knew he hadn't suffocated. I risked leaning closer. Moe sat quietly, nose and whiskers twitching, eyes wide, watching me. I hadn't noticed before how small his ears were, lying so close to his head. Couldn't believe I was even thinking it, but Moe was actually kind of *cute*.

Then I started worrying. What if he couldn't fend for himself out there in the wild? He was used to being fed at the sanctuary. If I set him free and he died, that definitely would bring a world of bad luck down on me. I sat there a while, with the rain pounding and the wipers *thwacking* and Moe's black nose twitching. I couldn't chance it. I couldn't let him go.

I had to take Moe home.

I drove back to my house and brought him inside. Having left the busted trapper cage in the woods, I decided to leave Moe in the cellar while I went out to buy a new cage. After I closed the door carefully behind me, I washed the mud off my hands, face, neck, and arms, put peroxide on my scratches and bandaged them, and then changed into dry clothes. I felt like a new man.

I headed out to an ATM, withdrawing the cash I'd need to pay anonymously. Then I drove two counties over, where no one would know me, and bought the biggest rabbit cage I could find. As I was wandering through the pet store, I realized I'd have to get food for Moe. The checker at my local market would look at me funny if I started buying fruits and vegetables, so I picked up a few bags of Rabbit Chow, figuring groundhogs would like the same healthy food that rabbits did. I also bought bedding, a water bottle feeder, and a rabbit, too, so not to look odd.

A few miles from my house, I set the rabbit free in a big field. I certainly didn't need two pets, and I hoped letting four rabbit feet hippity hop away would bring me more good luck. By the time I pulled into my long driveway, the rain was letting up, and I'd had a fine day, despite my busted knee, broken toe, and the scars surely forming on my face. I had followed through with my plan and had saved our town from years of bad winters. Heck, I'd be a hero if only I could tell people what I'd done.

I was humming as I started down the stairs to my cellar, cradling the large cage. When I reached the bottom step, I took in the room, gasped, and dropped the cage on my freaking toe. I screamed every curse I'd ever learned and made up a few new ones, too.

The cement floor was covered with shit. Holes marred the drywall and my grandparents' ratty, old sofa. And there was Moe, sitting on that sofa, looking happy as could be. He trotted over to me, as if he were glad I was home. I counted to ten to keep from strangling him. Then to twenty. At thirty-five I gave up, grabbed him, and shoved him in his new cage. I didn't want to think about how long it would take me to clean up the cellar and patch the walls.

Happy freaking birthday to me.

I trudged upstairs, my knee squawking and toe burning the whole way. I deserved a consolation dinner. I threw my favorite in the microwave. Hungry-Man fried chicken. While it nuked, I popped open a beer and turned on the TV just in time to watch the Yankees beat the Red Sox. Could this day get *any* worse? When the microwave dinged, I got my dinner, flipped to the local news, and learned that, oh, yes, it could. The lead story was about Moe being kidnapped. Holy crap, I didn't think it would make the news. The reporter said the cops had found a few muddy boot prints leading out into the woods near Moe's pen, but they had no other leads.

I swigged my beer, thinking things through, trying not to worry. No way they could find me. Or Moe. I just had to play it cool.

* * * *

I was Mr. Cool himself when I showed up at the diner the next morning for my usual weekend breakfast. Bobby already sat at the counter, chatting up Sally. I eased onto my regular stool, and they both stopped talking, staring at me. Not a good sign.

"What happened?" Sally finally said.

"You old dog," Bobby added.

Old dog?

Sally leaned toward me and lifted my chin, examining my bandaged face. My left cheek had puffed up overnight. I'd smeared Neosporin on the scratches, but I still looked like a chipmunk, or a groundhog, which was ironic.

"As a birthday gift to myself," I improvised, "I decided to replace some ancient carpeting in my bedroom. I got all scratched up from the carpet tacks as I was pulling the old rug up."

Sally glanced at Bobby, her head tilted, eyes narrowed. Then she focused on me again. "You got a hickey on your neck from carpet tacks?"

Crud. I'd forgotten about my neck.

"You old dog," Bobby repeated. "Who *is* she?"

Sally leaned closer. "C'mon, Gus. We're all friends. Who'd you spend your wild birthday night with?"

Wild sex. I nearly smacked my forehead. A much better story. I decided to go with it.

"Aw, you don't know her. Besides, I'm not the kinda guy to kiss and tell."

Bobby laughed. "Heck, it's been years since you kissed at all, as far as I know."

Sally barked out a laugh, too, and slapped the counter. "The usual, Gus?"

"Yep."

I breathed a sigh of relief as she stepped into the kitchen and Bobby dug back into his pancakes. Thank God that conversation was over.

Bobby kept smirking at me while he ate. I was feeling an odd mixture of pride and embarrassment when Sally came back and filled my coffee mug. "Well, if Gus's going to keep his lady love a secret, we'll have to get back to the next big news. You hear about Moe, Gus?"

I snorted. I'd prepared for this conversation, practicing while looking at myself in the bathroom mirror. "Yeah, I heard. Good riddance is all I have to say. That groundhog never brought us anything but bad weather."

I glanced casually at Sally and Bobby as Sally shook her head again. They didn't seem to think there was anything unusual about my response. Good.

"How can you be so mean, Gus?" Sally asked. "Moe's a poor, defenseless animal."

Hmph. Showed what she knew, I thought, gingerly fingering the bandage on my cheek.

"I bet it was some kids from Ethan Allen College," Bobby said, dragging a forkful of pancake through the puddle of maple syrup on his plate. "They're always playing pranks. You watch. Moe will be back home before you know it, right and ready to give us his prediction come next Groundhog Day."

I gulped down my coffee and didn't say a word. Though I did smile a little. *Sorry, Bobby. This time, you're wrong.*

* * * *

Next Groundhog Day, I set my alarm to go off early. As usual, I woke up happy. Bobby and Sally were convinced I was still dating my so-called secret lady because I'd stopped being such a sourpuss (Sally's term). I let them believe what they wanted. Truth was, I *had* fallen in love. With Moe.

Over the past few months, Moe had become my best friend. He'd been hibernating since late October, of course, but in the time he'd been awake, we'd had a lot of fun. We watched football and ate dinner in front of the TV. I even let him drink a little beer once. Okay, twice.

Around Thanksgiving, the town had given up on Moe. They'd gotten another groundhog to take his place. I didn't care. Only Moe and his ancestors had the power to cause long winters. This new groundhog was merely a pretender to the throne.

Still, I was curious how he'd make out.

The sky was beginning to lighten as I turned off the alarm clock and got dressed. I wandered downstairs, switched on my coffee maker, and turned on the early-morning local news. A crowd bundled up in coats, hats, and gloves had gathered at town hall, warming themselves around a fire barrel, while they waited for our mayor to appear with Missisquoi Morris, the new groundhog. I checked that the window curtains were firmly drawn and hurried down to the cellar. Moe was asleep in his cage, curled in the soft fleece blanket I'd bought him.

"Moe," I whispered, tapping his cage. "Wake up, Moe."

He stirred a bit. I reached into the cage and carefully stroked his bristly fur, repeating his name softly. Moe opened his eyes and blinked. I let out a contented sigh, lifted him out of the cage, and carried him upstairs.

A few minutes later, we were sitting on the couch by the big window, shooting the breeze, like old friends on a park bench. Moe was the silent type, but as he ate some Rabbit Chow and I drank my coffee, I filled him in on everything that had happened in the months since he went to sleep. He couldn't believe the town had replaced him either.

Meanwhile, the TV reporter covering our downtown festivities stood next to a mound of snow, blathering on about Morris as if he were a pedigreed pooch. Moe wrinkled his nose, disgusted. When the mayor finally came out to make his speech, he mentioned Moe, said everyone missed him. Moe appreciated the kind words, I could tell. I pulled Moe onto my lap, his long black claws wrapping around my fingers. We were both excited, waiting for the big moment.

The mayor lifted Morris out of a small cage and held him up. The crowd went wild, chanting "Morris, Morris," while Morris seemed to shiver, nervous. I'd be nervous, too, if I were him. The sun had come up a few minutes before. No clouds. No overcast. The mayor would have to announce that Morris had seen his shadow so we'd have another endless winter. The crowd wouldn't like that.

Moe and I leaned forward to listen.

"On this day, February 2nd," the mayor said, "it's my honor to tell the citizens of Missisquoi that appearances can be deceiving. It may be a beautiful, bright morning, but when he arose this morning, Morris did not see his shadow. Fellow citizens, we will have an early spring!"

An early spring. *An early spring.* I hadn't heard those words in so long that I felt like dancing around the room. I knew it didn't matter what Morris predicted. He didn't have Moe's special powers. But still, I was so happy.

"Did you hear that, Moe?" I held him up before me. "An early spring!"

Just then, my heat cycled on. The window curtains fluttered, and a bright ray of sunshine streamed through the gap. Moe turned his eyes away from the light, down toward the floor. And we both saw it at the same moment. Moe's shadow.

Nooooo!

Barb Goffman is the author of *Don't Get Mad, Get Even*, a collection of short stories published in 2013 by Wildside Press. She won the 2013 Macavity Award for best short story published in 2012, and she's been nominated twelve times for national writing awards—the Agatha (seven times), the Anthony (twice), the Macavity (twice), and the Pushcart Prize (once). Barb's an editor of the Chesapeake Crimes anthology series and recently opened a freelance editing service focusing on crime fiction (www.goffmanediting.com). You can learn more about her writing at www.barbgoffman.com.

VALENTINE'S DAY

SEEING RED

by Rosemary and Larry Mild

The doorbell rang. Elise Harrenton saved the accounting spreadsheet on her iMac and trotted to the front hall. A Fed Ex guy stood on the porch. She opened the door and signed for a nine-by-twelve tan bubble bag addressed to Mr. Charles Harrenton. Return address: Cartier Fifth Avenue.

Elise's heart quickened. Charles didn't often buy her presents, but the package was from Cartier. It had to be for her. She carried the package into the dining room, sat down in one of the upholstered chairs, and pulled the tab. Inside sat a long blue velvet box. Under it peeked out an elegant silver envelope. Her fingers tingled as she removed the velvet box. Setting it on the table, she sprang its catch.

Couched in white satin lay a pendant: a white-gold chain and an exquisite square-cut sapphire surrounded by diamonds. In the noonday sunlight, the gems winked at her with self-satisfied knowledge of their brilliance. Elise flipped her shoulder-length chestnut hair behind her right ear, a habit when she anticipated something special about to happen.

Reaching into the bubble bag for the silver envelope, she pulled it out, opened it, and read: "My darling Melanie. Thank you for the blissful Bermuda weekend. Your devoted Charles."

Elise's lean body grew rigid. She felt a burning in her belly, heartburn in her chest, her neck and face on fire.

She and Charles had never taken a trip to Bermuda! They'd barely traveled anywhere the past few years. He traveled all the time, working eighty-hour weeks running his Fortune 500 company. She'd put up with his insane schedule because she loved him. Only to find out that he loved someone else?

What had gone wrong? Didn't they have a secure marriage, with trust and all the rest, and even good sex? Every negative detail suddenly loomed as the villain. Was she spending too much time at the gym, carving her former plump self into a gaunt, athletic machine? Was it the faint varicose veins threading her thighs? Her smallish breasts? The fact that she'd miscarried twice and hadn't been able to conceive again?

Whatever *it* was, she hadn't seen it coming. And there was no use denying that Charles was still a stunning man at forty: six-two, with sandy hair and confident green eyes.

Elise stayed rooted to the chair for a long time, replaying in her mind the joke Charles had made of her life. What should she do? Confront him when he walked through the door tonight? Rant and rave? Throw things? Threaten divorce? It all sounded so clichéd. She deserved better.

At that moment she stopped brooding. Her breath quickened, and a seed began to germinate within the farthest reaches of her mind. Charles would be leaving in a few days for another month-long business trip, due to return home on Valentine's Day. She would have her gift ready for him when he returned. A gleeful smile crossed her face. Yes, it was time to redecorate.

But first she had an urgent task. She took the silver card down the hall to her office, photocopied it, and printed it out in color. For evidence. Whipping out her digital camera, she took two photos of the velvet box: the first one closed; the second one with the glorious pendant lying in the open box. She checked the two images, pleased that she had remembered to turn off the flash, enhancing the natural lighting and showing off the jewels to their best advantage.

Next, she jumped into her Porsche, zipped over to Office Depot, and bought a nine-by-twelve tan bubble bag, exactly like the one that had been delivered. Back home in the kitchen, she boiled water, and as the steam chugged out of the teakettle spout, she held the bubble bag from Cartier above the scalding puffs and steamed off the "From" and "To" labels. After allowing them to dry, she used thin coats of Elmer's Glue to affix them to the envelope she'd just purchased. Saying goodbye to the sapphire and diamonds, she snapped the box shut and tucked it inside the bag, along with the card. Sealing the bag with great care, she placed it on Charles's desk, under the pile of other mail that had arrived that day. Charles would probably kick himself when he came home tonight and realized he'd given Cartier his home address instead of his mistress's, but he'd also think Elise was too wrapped up in her accounting work to notice.

All the better for her plan.

Next she needed to do her research. She couldn't remember all the irritants that bugged her husband most. Maybe the Internet could help. Typing madly, she Googled "Phobias" and discovered a plethora of links, from simple definitions to studies in psychiatric and psychological journals. Scanning the websites, she singled several out. *Ereuthophobia. Ornithophobia. Pteridophobia.* Those three would needle him the most.

* * * *

February 14th dawned clear and cold, with brilliant sun. Charles returned late in the afternoon, catching a cab at the train station, looking forward to a relaxed evening with his single-malt scotch and the NBA on TV. But when the cab pulled up to 1577 Larkspurr Lane, he wondered whether he'd given the driver the wrong address. Their conservative black front door was now a screaming enamel red—like a hooker's nail polish. The door swung open before he had a chance to use his key. Elise greeted him with a mock pinup-girl pose, in a filmy red teddy. As he stepped into the foyer, setting down his briefcase and luggage, she threw her arms around his neck. "So glad you're finally home, darling. Happy Valentine's Day!"

He tried an appropriate response, but it just wouldn't come. "Elise. The front door. It's so…garish!"

"Darling, welcome to our new décor." She helped him off with his cashmere overcoat and hung it in the closet. "How was your flight, sweetheart? You look beat."

"Snow in New York. Delayed takeoff. Nasty turbulence. In other words, not so great. But seriously, what's with the door?"

Elise nuzzled his neck. "It's *feng shui*, darling. The Chinese spiritual forces of wind and water. A red door symbolizes welcome—harmony with the universe."

"*Feng* hooey is more like it." Charles shook his head, spotting the new floor: a dizzying array of red and orange irregular shapes. "Jeez, Elise, isn't this kind of busy for a front hall?"

"Not really. Mosaics are the 'in' thing now. They call this pattern Sunset Blitz." She led him into the living room. "Let me give you the tour, dear. Ta da! Our new contemporary home. Quite electrifying and exquisite, I think."

Charles's jaw dropped. He couldn't speak. His eyes ached from what he saw. A tomato-red leather sofa, flanked by matching bucket chairs. On a glass coffee table, a tall vase filled with long-stemmed red and salmon rosebuds. An area rug edged in a broad border of Chinese red. He gritted his teeth at the sight of the freshly painted walls: wide vertical stripes of ruby red and maroon. The motif continued down the hall to the kitchen. "I guess I can get used to this stuff, if I have to," he mumbled.

His agreeable mood lasted about five seconds, until he noticed the hanging pots of greenery in each corner of the living room: voluptuous ferns overflowing with coiled tendrils. An involuntary shudder shook his body. "What the hell, Elise. Those damned things look downright snaky!"

It was then that he heard a squawking commotion in the kitchen. He turned pale. "Birds? In this house?" He raced toward the kitchen and lurched to a stop in the doorway. A tall cage stood beside the breakfast table. Two large parrots swayed from side to side on their roosts. Their beady eyes stared at him as if he were an intruder.

Charles broke into an icy sweat. "Elise, have you gone totally around the bend?"

"Sorry, dear," she murmured. "I thought they'd lend a little amusement to our marriage. We can teach them to talk, you know, all sorts of cute things. They're very smart."

"Get those friggin' birds out of here! I'm going to change," he said, pressing his lips together to prevent escape of his ugliest thought. *If she's messed with our room, I'll strangle her.*

Charles entered the master bedroom, flicked on the light, and nearly fainted. He wished he were back on the road. The recessed lighting cast a sinister glow on the king-size bed. The headboard was covered in red and purple paisley; the comforter, shams, and sheets were scarlet, trimmed in purple. Vermillion curtains cascaded from ceiling to floor. And on the far wall, Elise had hung a large framed photo of parakeets.

Shivering, he tore off his business clothes and pulled on his favorite gray sweats. Would he at least be able to pee in peace? Opening the door to the master bath, he sighed with relief to discover the pristine white granite vanity top—until he saw that the shower walls were retiled in a throbbing red brick, and a potted fern sat perched on the toilet tank, its leaves curling—practically crawling—over the sides.

Dinner did nothing to soothe his anxiety. Crowded together on his Wedgwood plate were rare roast beef, a salad of grated red cabbage, and baby beets. Their juices, like blood, stained the mashed potatoes nestled against them. Famished as he was, Charles pushed the plate away. It wasn't just the nearly all-red meal. He couldn't tolerate individual foods touching each other. He desperately needed a glass of wine, but not the one she'd chosen for him: burgundy, in a gleaming blood-red goblet.

Elise handed him a long, slender box. *What can it be but a tie? How original is that?* And when he opened it, that's what it was. Tiny, white polka dots on crimson silk.

"Elise, what the devil's gotten into you?" Charles pounded the fuchsia tablecloth with his fist. "Have you ever seen me in a red tie? Well, have you?" His face contorted and his cheeks flushed.

A twinge of genuine sympathy clouded his wife's face. "No, darling, but I thought it would be a refreshing change. The stock market's been so bad, and the business news has been so gloomy. I thought this bright tie would cheer you up. It's an Armani, a special limited edition. I thought you'd like it. I'm sorry."

"Have you ever seen me in any suit or shirt or jacket that's not black, gray, navy, or brown?" He didn't wait for an answer. "I hate red! You know that. And what's with the ferns and the birds and this revolting dinner? Are you trying to drive me crazy?"

Charles suddenly bent over, clutching his stomach. "I don't feel so well. Something's wrong." He bolted from the table and staggered into the powder room. Falling to his knees, he flipped up the toilet seat and vomited. His guts heaved and retched until, finally, his belly quieted down. He flushed and pushed down the toilet-seat lid. Then his head began aching as he took in the lid's new cloth cover: red and yellow stripes. Pulling himself weakly upright to the vanity sink, he turned on the faucet to wash his hands and face. That's when he spotted the cerise hand towels and—in a crystal bowl—cherry-red, heart-shaped soaps. Charles broke into a spasm of chills. He reached for the bottle of Listerine mouthwash he kept handy, the citrus-flavored orange one. But what his eyes met with absolute horror was a bottle of Lavoris, in fire-engine red. Charles gasped and clutched his chest.

* * * *

Elise remained seated at the table, sipping her wine, smiling widely as she gazed at all the new touches in their house. *You deserve it, you louse, for cheating on me. And once your anxiety attack is over, I'll hand you the divorce papers—with a photo of that diamond-and-sapphire pendant attached. It should be enough to get me everything. Happy Valentine's Day.*

She strode to the powder room. The door was open. She arrived just as Charles swayed forward, backward, forward—and crumpled to the floor. His large frame filled the tiny room.

She knelt beside him. "Oh, my God! Wake up, dear. *Please* wake up. Are you all right?" But she knew he wasn't. His face had taken on a ghostly pallor. His eyes had rolled up into his head.

Elise felt a stab of remorse. Yes, she had orchestrated her scheme to feed on his phobias. Yes, she had intended to make him suffer an anxiety attack before serving him with divorce papers. But a heart attack? And one severe enough to kill her strong, handsome, robust husband? She hadn't intended to take her revenge so far.

Then she remembered the stunning pendant he'd bought for *someone else,* and her guilt evaporated as quickly as it had come. Everything was working out—amazingly well, actually. Charles's death was quite a bonus. A fortuitous accident! His generous life insurance policy would set her up in comfort. He hadn't bought the diamond-and-sapphire pendant for *her*, but so what? Now she could go out and buy herself one. Only bigger. *Happy Valentine's Day to me.*

On the way to the kitchen to call 9-1-1, Elise meandered through the rooms she'd transformed. In the dining room, pulsing with magenta accessories, a fresh thought hit her. Now she could get rid of the gauche décor, those violent, head-splitting reds. And the ferns. And those annoying parrots. Win. Win. Win.

Almost reluctantly, Elise made the call. And while she waited for the ambulance, she poured herself a large glass of white wine.

Rosemary and Larry Mild are cheerful partners in crime. They coauthor the Dan & Rivka Sherman Mysteries: *Death Goes Postal* and *Death Takes a Mistress*; and the Paco & Molly Mysteries: *Locks and Cream Cheese*, *Hot Grudge Sunday*, and *Boston Scream Pie*. They recently moved from Maryland to Honolulu and published *Cry Ohana*, a Hawaii thriller. Members of Sisters in Crime, both Chesapeake and Hawaii chapters, they have two wickedly entertaining stories in the anthology *Mystery in Paradise: 13 Tales of Suspense*. Rosemary also announces her new memoir: *Love! Laugh! Panic! Life with My Mother*. Visit the Milds at www.magicile.com.

PRESIDENTS' DAY

COMPROMISED CIRCUMSTANCES

by E. B. Davis

The Google Alert shocked me and brought back memories I'd tried to bury over thirty years ago. I leaned back in my desk chair and expelled a breath I'd been holding since college. I'd never told anyone what happened on Presidents' Day 1979, just a few months before graduation.

* * * *

It all started innocently enough the first week of freshman year. Although we were both from Pennsylvania, my roommate and I were from different backgrounds. Janice Butler came from the small town of Mercersburg, where her civil-engineer father worked. As a math major, she lived in the black-and-white world of equations and finite small-town values. My parents took over my grandfather's criminal law practice in Philadelphia, where I'd grown up. The private schools I'd attended with people from different races, cultures, and religions prepared me for the diversity I found in D.C. when I came to American University. During our freshman year, I remembered feeling as if Janice were a puppy I was training, teaching her about city living and the world of gray.

We went to a freshman mixer held in The Tavern, a bar in the student union. Back then beer was legal for eighteen-year-olds in D.C. We watched the crowd around us and sipped watery beer out of plastic cups.

At another table, an exotic-looking girl laughed. The laugh was distinctive, trilling as if it rolled off her tongue. Her kohl-lined eyes and dark, sleek hair made her appear older than the rest of us freshmen. Pressed Calvin Klein jeans encased her long, thin legs ending with strappy platform sandals that looked like expensive Italian leather. Janice noticed her, too, and I was surprised when she addressed the girl.

"Aren't you in my Intro Psych class?" Janice asked.

"Mondays at ten," the girl said, her accent soft and foreign. She got up and joined our table.

"Yeah, that's the section I'm in," Janice said. "Where are you from?"

"Originally Madrid, but I've lived in this country for years and went to high school in Bethesda. My father is with the Spanish Embassy."

"Wow, that must be exciting," Janice said.

"It's boring. I like the New York scene better," the girl said. "On weekends friends and I, we shuttle up there to party."

"Without your parents?" Janice asked.

I was suddenly embarrassed for Janice. I was afraid the girl would think Janice was a hick. How could I get her to shut up?

"Hi," I said, and stuck out my hand. "I'm Denise Kelly. I'm from Philly." I gestured to Janice and said, "This is my roommate, Janice Butler."

"Carmen Torres." She shook my hand, pressed her lips into a straight line, raised her eyebrows, and gave Janice a perfunctory nod.

"So, where do you go in the Big Apple?" I said.

"Studio 54, Max's Kansas City, CBGBs," Carmen said.

"Are you eighteen?" Janice asked.

Carmen nodded again as if talking to Janice were a chore, but she seemed so cool, I gave her a break. "This place must be killing you," I said, laughing.

"Meeting new people is cool, but this bar is a plebian drag."

"Do you live off campus?" Janice asked.

"I could have, but some friends and I got a quad in Anderson Hall."

"We're in Anderson too," I said, glad we had found something in common.

Carmen took out a cigarette, lit it, and blew out the smoke. "Let's go some place more happening. With drinkable wine," she added, grimacing at her plastic cup.

We left to pile into Carmen's new beige BMW, a car unknown to Janice, who asked Carmen a million questions about it. Carmen answered Janice's questions with a tight smile that I thought bordered on condescension.

Carmen headed toward Georgetown. I knew the way since I'd visited a prep school friend who went to Georgetown University. My friend had shown me around the area, pointing out the regular hangouts including her favorite, The Tombs.

As we rounded a traffic circle, Carmen's driving reminded me of a Le Mans driver. When she spoke of growing up in Madrid and then moving to D.C., she looked at us instead of the road. I held my breath as Carmen nearly sideswiped parked cars. She parked at a private residence, a tucked-away mansion with a driveway and garage, a sought-after commodity in an area crammed with shops and clubs loved by D.C. students.

"Are you allowed to park here?" Janice asked Carmen as we got out of the car.

"Of course. My parents own this house, silly."

The house was on Prospect Street, a block away from M Street, the main drag. I hoped Carmen wouldn't take the unfortunate shortcut down the hill to M Street, just to shock Janet, but as we approached the turnoff, I realized that was her plan.

"Carmen, let's just walk down 35th Street," I said, annoyed at her. As much as I wished Janice would shut up, I didn't want Carmen to pick on her.

"Oh, come on, it's fun."

"Oh, my God!" Janice gasped. "These are the steps from *The Exorcist*! I didn't know they were in Georgetown."

"Yes. It's a shortcut down to The Cellar Door," Carmen said. "I heard Jackson Browne might show up to play."

It was only one of the ways we could have gone down the hill to M Street, but I didn't want to chicken out. Carmen bounded ahead of us, scampering down the steep stairs. Janice clutched my arm as we gingerly descended the concrete steps on our platform heels while clinging to the black railing. Surrounded by a stone wall on one side and a house's brick façade on the other, the stairs amplified sounds from the street below with an eerie reverberation.

Through her sweatshirt I felt Janice tremble. The movie version of *The Exorcist*, released only two years before, was still scaring everyone so I couldn't fault her for fearing the steps. And given the darkness and our impractical footwear, they were treacherous. Headlights from cars turning left off the Whitehurst Freeway flashed in our eyes, blinding us. I tripped on my bell-bottoms, but Janice caught me. Midway down, Carmen screamed, frightening us half to death, then she looked back and laughed. I could have done without this drama. Carmen's lack of sensitivity started to repel me.

As we approached The Cellar Door, we saw the line snaking around the building. It looked like a private speakeasy I'd read about from the 1920s.

"We'll never get in," I said.

"No worries—I have connections." As Carmen passed those in line, they stared as if she might be someone famous. She stepped under the small canopy over the club entrance, opened the single metal door, and talked with a man. He ushered us in, making me feel conspicuous for butting in front of everyone, and directed us to the left where tables lined a wrought-iron railing overlooking the cellar stage.

As we waited for the show to start, Carmen gossiped about celebrities and places that were only names to me, and rolled her eyes at Janet's naïve comments. Strange that only a few hours before I was excited at having made such a cool new friend, and now I could hardly wait to get away from her.

At least one good thing came out of the experience. Janice and I bonded that night. When Carmen dropped us a few days later, we weren't surprised. And we didn't care.

* * * *

Fall semester of our senior year, Janice's little sister, Hadley, a high school senior, visited us to college-shop the university. Their parents allowed her to drive to D.C. without them since Janice could look after her. I found it interesting to compare the sisters. Hadley looked much like Janice, but she was less conservative and inhibited than Janice had been our freshman year. Like many older children, Janice must have been her parents' guinea pig. By the time Hadley came along, they were less fearful and strict. But Janice had come out of her shell, and showed her sister around campus and town like an old hand. I was proud of her.

We took Hadley with us to our usual Saturday night partying and three a.m. Sunday breakfast at an all-night diner. "You do this every weekend?" Hadley asked as she fingered the menu.

"Only for special occasions," Janice said. It wasn't entirely a lie. Now that we were seniors, with graduation looming, we'd cut back our clubbing a lot.

Hadley excused herself and went to the bathroom. The nearby booths were empty, so I took the opportunity to tell Janice about an embarrassing problem I'd hidden from her.

"My LSAT scores weren't good," I said. Attempting nonchalance, I buttered my toast.

"I'm sorry, Denise. Can you take them over?"

"These scores are higher than the last ones. The competition to get into law school is murder."

"I know. I've heard. Everybody majoring in Poli Sci seems to be applying. What are you going to do?"

I contemplated my plate to avoid looking her in the eye. "You know I've been going over to the law school and getting to know the admissions' staff."

"Yeah, but without high scores, what good will that do?"

"There's this young guy who works in admissions. He likes coke, and he's made it clear he'd like to go out with me."

"Denise, what are you thinking?"

"A lawyer needs to know when to switch tactics to win." I'd hoped to hear a resounding tone in my voice. Instead, I heard the outburst of billiard balls clashing from a strong break.

"So, like, he's going to change your scores?"

"Yes. He gets the scores from the College Board and enters them into their computer system."

"Won't they look at the hard copies?"

"He uses punch cards to enter the data and throws away the hard copies."

Janice stared at my face, and I felt her respect for me plummet.

"Don't look at me like that. You know my family expects me to join the family firm. I don't have any siblings. They expect me to take the law firm to the third generation and the next century. They paid for prep school and college. Conversation at family dinners all summer focused on me getting into law school. I can't disappoint them, and what else am I going to do?"

Janice answered by biting her lip. Damn. I hadn't wanted to keep such a big secret from my best friend, but now I saw confessing to her was a mistake.

It was still dark as we headed to the lot where I'd parked my car. Hadley walked on the street side, with Janice in the middle, as we rounded the corner to the parking lot behind the restaurant. I heard a woman's familiar laugh, a car door slammed, and then a car engine started. Tires squealed as a driver pulled out of a parking space on Wisconsin Avenue.

I startled when lights glared directly behind us as the car rounded the corner, and I jerked my head to look over my shoulder. The car ran over the curb onto the sidewalk, hitting Hadley from behind, catapulting her into the air, and sideswiping Janice, who rammed into me. As Janice fell onto the sidewalk, I ricocheted off Janice, pancaked into the wall of the restaurant, and avoided falling.

Hadley slammed with a thud onto the sidewalk. Face up. I ran over to her. Blood spattered the concrete behind her head. Her eyes were open but didn't move. When I talked to her and touched her shoulders, she didn't respond. As Janice picked herself off the sidewalk, I watched the car's rear lights fade as it sped down the road.

Janice hovered over Hadley, screaming. The restaurant manager and the waitress ran out. When the manager saw Hadley, he ran back inside to call for help. Suspecting that Janice was in shock, I forced her to sit on the sidewalk.

Soon the emergency response team came, but I knew before they started working on Hadley that she was dead. They medicated Janice, who was hysterical, while I told the police that Carmen was responsible. I'd heard her laugh. I'd seen her car.

* * * *

The scuttlebutt around the dorm later that morning put Carmen at a club with friends, partying and drinking. At around two a.m., they'd decided to go out for breakfast. Carmen's friends claimed that she intended to follow them to the diner, but she never arrived. No one, it seemed, saw her after that—until I spotted her car at the crime scene.

I tried to comfort Janice, but she froze me out. That afternoon her parents arrived. Janice left with them.

With everything that had happened, I didn't call my parents to tell them the news until two days later. The story shocked them.

"I'll have to testify against Carmen," I said. "It will be good for me to go through a trial and get experience in court. It's not the experience I wanted, but since I'm the only witness, I'll have to anyway."

"Will there even be a trial?" my mother asked.

Dumbfounded, I blinked and hesitated before saying, "Of course. She'll be charged with vehicular manslaughter and DWI."

"Are you sure?"

"Mom, she ran down Hadley and killed her. I saw her do it. Of course, she'll be tried."

"Honey, didn't you say Carmen's father was a diplomat."

"Yeah."

"Then she probably won't be charged with anything because she has diplomatic immunity."

"What? Her father maybe, but not her."

"Her, too. She's under twenty-three. Under the Diplomatic Relations Act, she has immunity."

My mouth hung open. I had trouble speaking. I told my parents I'd call them back. After debating for a few minutes, I called Janice's parents and asked for her. Even when she came to the phone, Janice sounded remote so I got down to the reason for my call.

"Have you heard from the cops?"

"Yes."

"When's the trial?"

"No trial," Janice said. "Carmen has diplomatic immunity. We can't even sue them. Carmen's father offered Dad $20,000 to cover Hadley's funeral expenses. Dad hung up on him." I heard a catch in her throat and an involuntary whimper come across the line. "I can't talk about it. I'll see you next semester, I guess."

She disconnected. I stood at the windows and stared at the parking lot.

* * * *

Janice returned to school at the end of January 1979, our last semester. She had changed again; turned taciturn. She hated the world, me included. We barely spoke, although I knew she overheard my call when I told my parents that I'd been accepted to law school. I sensed her disapproval, but she said nothing.

By mid-February, Janice's morose mood drove me insane. I sympathized, but living with her was hard. On the morning of Presidents' Day, the sky bore down in a gray mass. I felt claustrophobic in the dorm room.

"Let's get out of here," I said to Janice. "We could catch a holiday sale."

Janice shrugged as if she couldn't care less.

"Maybe later," she said. "I have to go to the library."

"If you're not up for shopping, let's go to Hamburger Hamlet for dinner, then catch a concert at the Cellar Door. We have to get out of here for a while before I scream."

Janice returned by four p.m. We piled on our winter coats and escaped outside. Snow had started falling so we took her car, which was outfitted with snow tires.

Having lived in Washington, D.C., for four years, I'd discovered the town's southern roots appeared during snowstorms. The residents raided grocery stores upon the mere threat of snow, maybe due to the city's haphazard snow-removal services. Seemingly intelligent residents drove in a brainless panic when it snowed. We found no line at Hamburger Hamlet.

By seven p.m., we parked below M Street on 33rd and made our way to the Cellar Door. There were a few inches of snow on the ground as we trudged uphill. I knew Janice was making an effort to act normally. We made small talk as we crossed over M Street and walked to the club. I wondered if we'd get in, but we'd arrived early, and the snow kept kids away. The doorman led us to a table at street level overlooking the stage below. Before we sat down, he warned us that they were recording that night, a live performance of George Thorogood and the Delaware Destroyers with a D.C. band called the Nighthawks.

We were starting to relax when I saw Carmen sitting at a table downstairs on the stage level. Janice spotted her, too. Her entire body stiffened as if she'd developed rigor mortis.

Janice clenched her fist around a napkin and squeezed. "It looks as if she's having the time of her life."

"I can't believe it," I said.

"Can't believe what?"

"I still can't get my head around her immunity—that she'll never go on trial—that she doesn't have to pay for—"

"Killing my sister?"

"Yeah." I looked down at the table. "Had it been either one of us, we'd be in the slammer right now, and our folks would be broke from losing a civil lawsuit."

"Yes. Our lives and our family's lives would be ruined," Janice said. "As they are now, but we're the victims—not the perpetrators." Her eyes spoke of hurt, anger, but there was more inside her.

I understood and looked away, impotent from the injustice of it all. "Do you want to go?"

"No, I have to deal with this, but I need to take a walk alone. Do you mind?"

"No. I understand. You'll be back?"

"Yeah," Janice said. She got up and walked out the door.

I waited in the bar listening to the music, ordered another drink, and watched Carmen and her friends enjoying themselves. I spent the evening clenching my teeth. When the concert ended, it was late. Janice still hadn't returned to the bar. I figured she'd walked back to the car and was waiting for me.

As I stood up and put on my coat, Carmen and her group slithered out the door. I followed, intent on studying an inhuman curiosity or perhaps a subhuman creature. Was she acting or had she no conscience?

Several inches of snow covered the streets and sidewalks. Few cars were on the road. Carmen and her friends jaywalked across M Street, turning toward 34th. Their gaiety sickened me. I followed, ducking into a storefront when they paused at a car. Carmen refused a ride and bid the others good night.

"I'll be fine," she said. "I'll sleep at my parents' house," I overheard her telling them.

As the car left, Carmen continued down 34th Street, walking very slowly—almost staggering. Since it was on my way too, I continued to follow her about a half block behind. When she took a left on the C&O Canal path, I was surprised since most women kept on the street for safety, but a few overhead lights lit the path well enough to see the falling snow. I understood then why Carmen chose the path. It was bucolic and serenely quiet in the snowfall. The sound of our muffled steps hovered above silence. My ears still rang from the loud music in the bar. I was sure Carmen had no idea that I was following her.

In the middle of the block, a recessed building's remote lights obscured visibility. Farther along the path, the lights resumed. As Carmen walked through the dim area, a figure jumped out from the recessed building and hit her over the head with what looked like a metal bar. I stopped, shocked, and stood monument-still.

Carmen screamed as she fell face-first onto the snowy path. The attacker was quickly upon her, pressing her face into the snow and silencing her scream. Carmen struggled. I watched and recognized the attacker. Janice put her boot on the back of Carmen's neck and whacked her head again with the metal bar. Carmen no longer moved, but Janice hit her again and again, and then she pushed Carmen off the path and down the canal's bank.

Janice must have sensed my presence because she walked toward me into the light. She looked me in the eyes and said, "You say a word and I'll ruin you."

She turned and ran toward 33rd Street, where we'd parked her car. I started to follow and realized that I'd have to pass by Carmen's body. My boots' prints would be pressed into the snow. I retreated the way I'd come and went the long way around. When I returned to where we'd parked, Janice's car was gone.

I saw Carmen's BMW parked a few cars up the street. Janice must have returned to her car, noticed Carmen's car nearby, and decided to lie in wait for her. The opportunity must have been too tempting. The metal bar she had struck Carmen with could have been the tire iron from her trunk.

I walked back up to M Street, telephoned my friend at Georgetown U from a bar, and stayed the night with her. It snowed through the next day, accumulating to over eighteen inches. Classes were canceled.

I never saw Janice again. When I returned to the dorm, the resident assistant asked me to pack Janice's stuff. She told me that Janice had decided to withdraw from school, go home, and get grief counseling. I packed her stuff. One day, it disappeared.

No one discovered Carmen's body until the snow melted a week later. The police never contacted me. I figured by the time they realized the path was a crime scene our boot prints were trampled or melted. Janice probably threw the tire iron into some Pennsylvania backwoods.

* * * *

Thirty years later I was nearing retirement and Carmen's murder case was still open on the D.C. police books. I'd always been curious about Janice and eventually placed her name on my Google Alert list. I still wondered why Janice felt she had to threaten me back then. After what Carmen had done, I would have kept her secret.

The alert, when it came, took me to an article describing how she'd recently established a scholarship fund for crime victims. I wondered why now, after all these years. Then I realized her parents, like mine, must have died and left her money.

I packed up my laptop and felt the hollowness of the empty office that I'd inherited from my parents and grandfather. Between these walls I'd built cases, defending every kind of lowlife. Memories echoed back at me from empty rooms.

Since Janice still went by her maiden name, I wondered if she, too, hadn't married. My long-time romantic partner had retired to Virginia, and I planned to join him. Retiring my shingle and starting again without my parents' expectations made me feel released from a prison sentence. I hoped Janice's generosity redeemed her.

Chesapeake Crimes: This Job is Murder presented E. B. Davis's short story "Lucky in Death." In the *He Had It Coming* anthology, a kidnapped dental hygienist wins in "The Acidic Solution." A young thug proves no match for a chemo patient/mother in "No Hair Day," contained in A *Shaker of Margaritas: Bad-Hair Day*. On the cusp of adulthood, runaway Shannon finds that if you care, leaving isn't an option in *Fish Nets'* "The Runaway." Look for "The Ice Cream Allure" a romantic mystery spoof contained in *Carolina Crimes: Tales of Lust, Love, and Longing*. She blogs at http://writerswhokill.blogspot.com.

ST. PATRICK'S DAY

I WILL SURVIVE

by Shaun Taylor Bevins

"I'm gonna kill him, Shauna."

"Personally, I've always felt that the punishment should fit the crime. So I vote for castration. Now that would send a clear message."

Emily stared down at the size-six, hot-pink, satin thong she'd found under the seat of her Camry a week after lending it to Jeff, her boyfriend of two years. Her cheeks burned as she imagined him slipping them off some tattooed buxom bimbo with a nose ring and a bad dye job, sprawled across her four-month-old leather seats.

"Bastards, Shauna. All men are two-timing bastards."

"No, Em, not all men, just the ones you date."

Emily tossed the panties on her kitchen counter with a sigh. Though she knew Shauna had always disliked Jeff and couldn't be objective about this newest development in their relationship, her best friend was right.

"Em, when it comes to choosing men, you have a permanent handicap," Shauna was saying. "A severe case of bad taste, with a definite touch of no self-control. Even back in junior high with—what was his name—Stephen? The one with eyeliner and more jewelry than both of us put together."

Emily said nothing, hoping Shauna would run out of steam.

"And then Brad, the football player." Shauna was counting on her fingers. "Just the kind of boy mothers adore and fathers invite over to watch the game. Did your parents ever figure out what he was doing to you after they shuffled off to bed? And then when you got to college, Alan 'the porn king' Pinkerton, and Amit 'oops, I forgot my wallet again' Rajav?"

Emily thought Shauna was being unfair, bringing up mistakes she'd made due to youth and inexperience. Though she didn't have that excuse now. Damn it, things were supposed to be different with Jeff. Emily was an adult now, a successful, twenty-six-year-old personal trainer who'd recently opened her own small studio in Annapolis, Maryland. And he was a third-year Emergency Room resident doctor with a promising future at Baltimore's Mount Sinai Hospital. Everything had looked golden.

Then she'd discovered the thong. She was still in shock.

"Can we skip all that?" she said. "And I'm not sure I'm up for drinks at O'Malley's. I know tonight was supposed to be a girls' night, but I need time to think. Figure out what to do next. You understand."

"Yeah, I understand. You're actually considering giving that creep a chance to explain."

"That's not fair, Shauna."

"I'll tell you what's not fair: borrowing you girlfriend's car to pick up some bimbo, doing her in the backseat, and then lacking the decency or the brains to make sure she takes her dirty panties with her."

"You know, Shauna, sometimes I really hate you."

"Because you know I love you and I always tell the truth. Now it's Friday night and St. Paddy's Day to boot, and I'm not going out without my best friend."

Emily tapped her slender fingers on the counter, glaring at the panties. "Fine, but not O'Malley's. Nine o'clock at Barkley's; it won't be as crowded. And just a few drinks and no one else. I'm not in the mood for socializing."

"That's my girl."

"At least I'm still somebody's girl."

"Em, you do realize he doesn't deserve you?"

* * * *

Only a quarter 'til nine and Barkley's was already jammed. The lead singer of a local band belted out the chorus of Def Leopard's "Pour Some Sugar on Me" as tightly packed, glistening bodies gyrated in unison on the tiny parquet dance floor. The place smelled like a cocktail of stale beer, fresh sweat, and tonight's special, corned beef and cabbage. Emily nudged her way through the dense crowd to the bar, hoping to find Shauna already there and waiting with a drink.

"Over here, Em. Over here."

Emily spied Shauna standing beside a corner booth. She sidled past a constellation of boisterous college boys who barely looked old enough to vote, let alone drink.

On the other side, Shauna greeted her with a Corona. She was all dolled up in a rust-colored camisole and a thigh-length tan suede skirt that showcased her generous curves and the toned slender legs of a dedicated runner. She looked dressed to kill, with nearly every eligible red-blooded guy and perhaps even a few bi-curious women in the joint her potential victims.

"I thought we agreed, only a few drinks. Alone." Emily gestured toward her friend's sexy outfit.

"What? So just because Jeff-the-jerk finally lived up to your low expectations, you want to take it out on me and my choice of fashion?"

Emily shook her head. "Sorry, you're right. Plus, with that body, you'd look hot in sweats, so what's the difference. Clearly, I'm jealous." She gestured at her own petite five-foot-three frame, clad in a simple white T-shirt and slender-cut blue jeans. Though her olive complexion, full lips, and big chestnut-brown eyes had their own allure, her curves were subtle and not even a padded, push-up bra could boost her bosom into Shauna's league.

Shauna tilted her head and extended her arms. "Now come here, sweetie. That sleaze you call a boyfriend is scum and ain't nothing that a hug from your best bud Shauna and a few more of these can't fix." She held out the Corona.

Two beers later, Emily had cried and laughed, but she still couldn't help dwelling on Jeff's infidelity.

"So who do you think the thong belonged to?" she asked.

Shauna shrugged.

"A nurse from work, right?" Emily suggested. "You know the cast of characters better than I do, now that you're working in the hospital's drug dispensary. What do you think?"

Shauna shrugged again.

The band took a break, and Shauna finished off her drink. Emily looked around for their waitress but instead caught an unexpected glimpse of *his* profile. Her stomach did a complete somersault.

"Oh, my God. Don't look now but—"

Before Emily could finish, Shauna had followed her eyes to a trio of males that included her friend's soon-to-be ex.

"You've got to be kidding me," Shauna said. "Jeff? Here? What are the chances..." Without finishing, she glared at Emily. "Please, tell me you didn't know, Em."

"I have just as much right to be here," Emily protested. "Plus, I didn't know. Not really. Just because he hangs out here on occasion doesn't mean he'd be here tonight. I thought he'd be at the hospital."

"Emily!" Shauna's voice resonated through the bar. Jeff and several nearby patrons glanced in their direction. Shauna raised her hand to hide her face.

"Shit, girl. I'm so sorry."

Emily simply shrugged. The confrontation had to happen. Might as well take place while she still had a couple of beers and Shauna's pep talk to get her courage up.

"Hey, babe," Jeff said, leaning over to kiss Emily's cheek. A whiff of his aftershave sparked memories of an intimate nature, memories that made her cringe now that she knew the truth. "Happy St. Paddy's Day."

Emily forced her lips into a smile.

"Thought you guys were hanging out at O'Malley's tonight," he added.

Emily felt sick.

"Is everything okay, babe? You don't look so well."

Shauna mumbled something under her breath while rolling her eyes, and Emily shot her a warning look.

Turning back, she stared up at Jeff. She wasn't the only one who didn't look so well. The start of a bristly shadow covered his usually clean-shaven face. Add to that his tousled hair and wrinkled shirt and Jeff appeared tired, exhausted even. "Listen, Jeff, we need to talk," she said, placing her trembling hand over his.

His brows pinched together in a serious expression. "Sure, babe. We can talk."

He glanced over at his friends, Todd and another guy she didn't recognize, a tall, broad-shouldered stranger with a scraggly goatee and wisps of sandy-blond hair sticking out from under his faded Orioles cap. Todd's eyebrows lifted as if to say, "What's up, bro?" and the dude with the goatee pointed to his watch.

Jeff glanced over at Shauna, who was still staring down at her drink with her usual air of contempt. "Let's talk," he said. "But not here."

By the time they stepped onto Baynard Street, Emily's nerve was fading. Why did Jeff have to be so damned GQ? Even unkempt as he was tonight, he exuded pure, physical sex appeal. Maybe he did deserve a second chance. She hadn't heard his side of the story. There could be a logical explanation for the panties.

Yet when Jeff reached over and tried to hold her hand, she flinched.

"I know all about her," she blurted, ripping her hand away.

"Know all about who?"

Emily's shaking hand plunged into her purse and emerged gripping the pink undergarment as well as a tube of Coffee and Crimson lipstick that tumbled to the pavement and rolled into the street. She wasn't sure why she had brought the panties along. Maybe it had been an accident. Or maybe subconsciously she had anticipated running into Jeff. Either way, with the accused acting as if nothing had happened, she was glad she had the evidence ready.

"These," she said, shoving the undergarment toward his face. "How in the hell do you explain these?"

Shuffling back, Jeff grabbed the panties and held them up with both hands. "Well, not that I'm an expert on women's underwear, but I think they call this little number a thong. So if you're asking my opinion, let me go on record as saying I prefer those black, lacy things you had on the other night."

Emily snatched the thong back. "You're making jokes. You think this is *funny*? You're an even bigger jerk than I imagined." She drew back her hand, still holding the thong, to slap him. He grabbed her wrist.

"Whoa there, Em. I don't know what this is all about, but I think it's time for you to tell me exactly what's got your panties all bunched up. Forgive the pun."

His joke was the final straw. "It's over, as in I'm over you. How's that for an explanation?" She spun around and plowed back through a crowd of smokers toward the pub until Jeff seized her arm.

"Let go of me," she demanded. "You're hurting me."

"I'm not letting go until you explain what the hell has gotten into you besides too much alcohol."

Tears welled up in Emily's eyes. She threw the panties, and they landed on his shoulder. "These are what has gotten into me. I found them in my car."

With a look of befuddlement, Jeff removed the thong clinging to his corduroy shirt. Either he was the best liar she had ever met or he really didn't comprehend where she was going with this.

"In the back seat."

Still nothing.

"After *you* borrowed it."

Suddenly, a look of enlightenment flashed over his face.

"Em, you don't honestly think…I mean you couldn't possibly believe that I…and in your car for Christ's sake? What kind of lowlife do you think I am?"

Exactly! Emily bit the inside of her bottom lip. Perhaps if she hadn't had the evidence with her she might have expected a denial, but seriously, who did he think he was fooling?

"Listen, Em. These aren't mine."

"Well of course they're not yours. Hell, I think I could handle it if they were yours."

Jeff smiled and again his cavalier attitude drew Emily's wrath.

"How can you make light of this? Seriously. I trusted you." Defeated and on the verge of tears, she looked down and whispered, "You were supposed to be different from the others." Emily was crying now, and this time when Jeff took her hand, she didn't resist. Instead she melted into his arms, burying her head in that comfortable nook between his shoulder and chest.

"Em, I swear on my life, I have no idea where this thong came from. You've got to believe me. I borrowed your car, drove it to work, and then drove it home. It sat in the parking garage all night until I returned it to you the next day." He reached down and cradled her chin, gently forcing her head up until their eyes met. "You're it for me." He pinched her chin gently between his thumb and forefinger as if for emphasis. "Understand? You, nobody but you."

Emily wanted to believe him. Her heart said yes, but her head kept bringing up her questionable track record with men. She had a knack for picking losers. Why should Jeff be any different simply because he was beautiful and signed the initials M.D. after his name?

He stroked her cheek. "We're going to figure this out," he reassured her, his voice taking on a graver quality, a seriousness that gave Emily the eerie feeling he wasn't merely referring to the thong and their relationship. "But right now I've got to get back to the bar. There's a guy there waiting on me, someone I've got to talk to. It's important."

"And I'm not."

"Of course you're important. But so is this. You're just gonna have to trust me."

Trust. Wasn't that the whole problem?

"Who's the guy?" she asked, remembering the dude with the goatee, not a clean-cut, academic type Jeff usually hung out with.

"Just a co-worker."

"Hospital business in the pub?"

"It's a long story, but I promise we'll discuss all this later."

Emily's head hurt. Her earlier buzz had worn off, and now she needed either the consolation of another drink or the comfort of her bed. The first wasn't an option. A paradox of jumbled thoughts, she needed time to think and suspected she'd have more clarity after a good night's sleep.

Jeff escorted her to her car. With her back against the Camry, he leaned into her, and the familiar weight of his body made her want to fling her arms around him and pretend none of this had ever happened. She could hear Shauna's disapproval in her head, but it wasn't her fault. Jeff made her whole body tingle.

"You okay to drive?" Jeff asked.

Emily nodded.

Cupping her head with both hands, he guided her face toward his and kissed her. She didn't reciprocate, but she didn't resist.

"Jeff," she called as he hurried off to the entrance. "If Shauna's still there, tell her I'm sorry and that I'll call her tomorrow."

Jeff raised his arm and gave her the thumbs up.

* * * *

The knocking at the door woke Emily. Sunlight poured in through her bedroom window. She squinted in order to see the clock. Ten after eleven. Had she really slept that long? Her mouth felt pasty, and when she sat up a mild wave of nausea made her pause while it passed. What on earth had she been thinking, two beers on an empty stomach, and then half a bottle of wine after she got home? Of course then it hit her like a severe case of the shits. She'd been thinking about her two-timing boyfriend.

The knocking at the door continued. "I'm coming," she yelled then cringed at her own voice.

"Em, it's me. Open up."

Shauna. She'd called her friend's cell phone when she'd gotten home, but there had been no answer. At the time, she wasn't too concerned. But now with Shauna frantically knocking at the door, her pulse raced.

"Coming. I'm coming."

She slipped on a pair of fluffy slippers and then proceeded downstairs. Each step sent another wave of nausea rippling through her. At the bottom of the stairs, she briefly caught her reflection in the mirror. She looked like a corpse.

When she opened the door, it worried her to see Shauna looking almost as ragged as she did.

"Jeez, what's wrong?" Emily asked.

"Oh, thank God. Then you haven't heard?" The possibility seemed to make Shauna calmer.

"Heard? Heard what?"

"You better sit down. It's Jeff."

"Is he okay?"

"No," she said. "He's gone. He took an overdose of codeine."

By the time Shauna had told her the details, Emily felt as though the breath had been sucked from her lungs. Suicide? Could it be true? She closed her eyes and tried to imagine the sensation of Jeff's weight pressed against her body as he tenderly kissed her on the mouth, his smell filling her head with thoughts she didn't want to admit, especially to herself. How could someone so alive just hours before be dead? And not just dead, dead as the result of an overdose. Dead, as in really dead. The word stuck in her mouth like a bad aftertaste, and she couldn't bring herself to say it.

"Just one last thing, Em," Shauna added, interrupting her thoughts.

Emily glared up at her friend. There couldn't possibly be more.

"I hate bringing this up now, but better you hear it from me."

Emily's balled-up fists clenched the bottom of her nightshirt.

"They, the police, found some things in his bedroom."

"Things? What sort of things?"

Shauna glanced down at the floor. "A woman's negligee."

This time, the wave of nausea actually made Emily gag. She wanted to claim the negligee was hers. She couldn't. She rarely slept at the uncomfortably small apartment Jeff shared with an equally low-paid fellow resident. When they slept together it was in her townhouse. There was no way the negligee could be hers.

She drew her knees into her chest and rocked back and forth, trying to make sense of it all. The thong, the pills, the suicide, the negligee.

"But Shauna," she said after she'd had a few moments to digest it, "how do you know all this? Maybe you're wrong."

"Oh, sweetie, I wish I was." Shauna reached out and slid her arm across Emily's shoulder. "Last night I had to finish up some paperwork at the hospital. Tina, the pharmacy tech on duty, is dating a police officer. The weight-lifter type with the mermaid tattoo? I introduced you to him at Troy's barbeque over Labor Day." Emily nodded and motioned Shauna to keep going. "Anyway, he shows up shortly after I do and starts to tell Tina about his last call. Said some guy called 9-1-1 after coming home from his shift at the hospital and finding his roommate unconscious."

"Unconscious." Emily realized that she sounded hopeful, as if she didn't already know the outcome.

"Yes, sweetie. He was still breathing when they found him. They tried pumping his stomach, but…"

Emily gasped as she imagined Jeff's colleagues, men and women she had likely met at some social function, trying desperately to save one of their own.

"It was Jeff," Shauna continued. "I went down to the ER myself. I had to find out for you."

Emily's whole body went numb. Shauna stroked her hair.

"One last thing, Em. The police will need to talk to you."

"To me?"

"You're Jeff's girlfriend. Don't worry. Everything's going to be okay. I promise."

Shauna's arm tightened around Emily, who again felt thankful for her best friend. At least she wouldn't have to face this nightmare alone.

* * * *

The coroner's office eventually ruled Jeff's death a suicide. On the morning of St. Patrick's Day, the hospital had suspended Jeff, pending further investigation of his role in a case involving inappropriate behavior with a female patient. The guy with the goatee at the bar, a young nurse's aide assigned to the ER, was later accused of touching and filming a sedated patient's breasts. One of Jeff's patients. Had Jeff participated in the molestation? Or was he, as chief resident, merely guilty of neglect for not following up and properly reporting the rumors that such a video existed? What was behind that meeting in the bar—was he confronting the guilty aide with his crimes? Or making sure he and his partner in crime had their stories straight?

Four months after Jeff's death, Emily still didn't know and had to accept that she probably never would. And while Jeff had never seemed suicidal, he came from three generations of doctors. Medicine wasn't just Jeff's job, it was his life. Maybe the prospect of losing the right to practice could push even someone as stable as her ex-lover to desperation.

At least the police had never identified the owner of the negligee, saving Emily the humiliation of their friends learning Jeff had been unfaithful. In fact, his suicide had saved her the humiliation of a break-up, and in that small way she felt Jeff had made some small retribution for his indiscretions. Rather than being pitied and whispered about behind her back, she was treated with respect as the innocent, bereaved girlfriend. The only person who knew better was Shauna, who would never tell.

Emily was adjusting the calla lilies and a few sprigs of baby's breath in a flower arrangement when a car horn jolted her from her reverie. Shauna was right on time. Carrying the flowers, Emily headed outside, opened the back door of Shauna's Mazda, and secured the arrangement. Emily knew Shauna thought she was overly sentimental, especially considering Jeff had cheated on her. In Shauna's mind, he got what he deserved. "Karma," she'd say whenever Emily started to over-romanticize the relationship. But she'd agreed to stop by the cemetery on their way to a wine festival, so Emily could leave the flowers on Jeff's grave. Emily's heart rose a little, knowing she had a best friend who would always be so considerate of her.

During the drive to the cemetery, a steady stream of classic rock took the place of conversation. Shauna waited in the car listening to the music while Emily visited Jeff's gravesite. It had been almost a month since her last visit, and the previous bouquet had turned brown and withered in the summer heat. She felt a little guilty for not coming sooner. She exchanged the fresh flowers for the dead ones, letting out a long deep sigh. She wished she had something to say, but knew it had all been said before, so instead she just pulled a few weeds that had sprung up around Jeff's tombstone and returned to the car.

A little later they stopped at a gas station, and Shauna went in for snacks and a bathroom break. She left the key in the ignition so the radio continued to sing out familiar tunes in her absence, typical thoughtful behavior for Shauna. Everything was going great until Survivor's "Is This Love" played out over the car's speakers. It was the first song Emily and Jeff had ever danced to. She didn't want to cry, but after the cemetery, the impulse was simply too strong. She burst into sobs. She searched her purse for some Kleenex to blow her nose. When none could be found, she tried the glove compartment, hoping for at least a napkin.

Unlike the spotless interior of the car, the glove compartment was cluttered, jammed full with lipsticks, maps, sunglasses, and slips of paper that spilled out as soon as she opened it. Emily was collecting the loose pieces of paper, including receipts and even a few parking tickets, when one of them caught her eye, a piece of notepaper with a list scrawled on it in red marker:

Percocet
Vicodin
Oxycontin
Codeine

The first three lines had been crossed out. Codeine had been circled several times in overlapping strokes.

Emily stared out the window, then back down at the paper. Codeine, the same drug that had killed Jeff. What could it mean? Shauna had always disliked Jeff. And she had access to codeine at the hospital. And Jeff hadn't seemed suicidal....

Emily shook her head. Shauna was a pharmacist. She probably had lists like this sitting all around at work. Codeine was a popular drug.

Just then Emily noticed Shauna walking back toward the car, a coffee in each hand. She crammed the papers back into the compartment and slammed it shut. Still tissue-less, she sniffed hard and wiped whatever was left behind on her sleeve. Desperate times required desperate measures.

"Hey," Shauna said, climbing into the Mazda. "Two creams, no sugar." She handed Emily one coffee.

Emily felt like such a traitor. How could she have allowed such awful thoughts into her head? Shauna was her friend, her best friend: the kind of friend who would do anything for her. It was a coincidence. Plain and simple. Clearly the visit to the cemetery had affected her judgment. She wasn't thinking rationally. She sipped her coffee and sloshed the warm silky liquid back and forth in her mouth, trying to focus on the rural scenery outside, but she just couldn't stop thinking about the list no matter how hard she tried.

"Hey, Shauna," she said, when she could no longer keep her thoughts to herself, "I've been meaning to ask you something."

"I figured. You looked as if your brain had shifted into overdrive. Shoot, sweetie."

"I was just thinking about the suicide."

Shauna's expression soured. "Aw, come on, Em. It's been four months. I kind of understand this whole ritual with the flowers and the cemetery, honestly I do. But eventually you're going to have to let it go. Jeff's gone."

Suddenly Emily felt on the defensive. She knew that Shauna disapproved of her visits to Jeff's gravesite, and she especially disapproved of the flowers.

"Listen. It's not that you shouldn't grieve," Shauna was saying. "Grieving is natural, but this, this whole thing, this is way beyond grieving. You're idealizing Jeff and your relationship, remembering them both as something they weren't."

Emily frowned. She wasn't in the mood for a lecture. "I really don't think you can be objective," she muttered, more out of spite than anything.

"Excuse me?" Shauna said.

"Oh, never mind."

The next several miles passed in a stiff, uncomfortable silence. Then at a stoplight, Shauna reached over and placed her hand over Emily's. "After everything that's happened, you have to realize he didn't deserve you. He was a jerk, a criminal even."

"They never proved—" Emily began to say, but Shauna didn't let her finish.

"Please, Em. Save it. You can't fool yourself forever, and you certainly can't fool me. Even if he wasn't involved in the videotaping, he was a narcissist. And the worst thing is that he would've married you. He would've married you and dedicated the rest of his life to making you miserable, and judging by how you've been acting these past few months, you would have let him." Shauna held up her hand when Emily opened her mouth to offer a rebuttal. "Don't even try to pretend you would've ever left him. I know you, Em. You would have stayed, made excuses, idealized the good times no matter how few or infrequent they might be, just as you're doing now. Don't look at me like that. You may think this sounds horrible, but I think his death is the best thing that ever happened to you."

Emily couldn't believe what she was hearing. "You're actually saying that you're glad he's dead?"

Shauna's eyes stayed focused on the road. "Yes. When I think about what he would have put you through eventually, yes."

Emily didn't know how to respond.

"I'm saying this as your friend," Shauna added. "Someone who realizes just how special you are. Someone who will always do everything she can to protect you."

Emily could feel herself starting to tear up.

* * * *

A little before midnight, on their way home from the wine festival, Shauna pulled into a rest stop. "If you gotta go, this is it till we get home."

"Nah," Emily said. "I'm good."

As soon as Shauna's silhouette vanished from her field of vision, Emily ripped open the glove compartment, fished out the list she'd found earlier, and slid it into her back pocket.

Shauna returned minutes later. "Ready?" she asked, opening a pack of Ritz peanut butter crackers that she must have bought from a vending machine inside. She offered Emily a cracker.

"Actually, Shauna, I think I'll pass on the crackers, thanks." Emily pointed to her bloated stomach. "Too much wine and cheese. But I probably should use the bathroom while we're here."

Her grinning mouth full of crackers, Shauna made a shooing motion.

The rest stop was almost deserted. Emily entered one of the restroom stalls and locked the door. She slipped the piece of paper out of her pocket and stared at it for a moment. She could follow the trail it suggested. Try to find out where Shauna had gone on St. Paddy's Day, after Emily went home. Ask around the hospital to see if any codeine had disappeared from the pharmacy where Shauna worked. Peek in Shauna's file drawers to see if she'd made any charges at Frederick's of Hollywood around mid-March.

Or she could trust that Shauna had better judgment than she did. That whatever Shauna had done was for her best friend's sake.

Without another thought, she threw the list into the toilet and flushed. Shauna was right. Emily did deserve better. She had always deserved better. Jeff, on the other hand, was scum and had gotten exactly what he deserved.

She had to believe that.

"So," Shauna said, after Emily climbed back into the car. "Are we ready now?"

"We sure are," Emily said. Several minutes later, when Gloria Gaynor's "I Will Survive" came on the radio, Emily turned up the volume, and they both sang along. Mid-chorus, Emily glanced over at

Shauna, who crooned the catchphrase words with conviction, to which she raised her own voice. Though she might have crappy taste in men, she sure knew how to pick her friends, and thanks to her best friend, Shauna, she *would* survive without Jeff.

Some of her future boyfriends might not survive, but she would.

Shaun Taylor Bevins is an aspiring writer, voracious reader, mother, wife, scientist, and teacher. When asked the all-revealing question, "Cats or dogs?" she answers, "Both!" She's especially honored to be included in this Sisters in Crime anthology. You can learn more about her at her website www.broadneck-writersworkshop.com.

TALK LIKE A PIRATE DAY

(September 19th)

DEAD MEN TELL NO TALES

by Cathy Wiley

"Your wench is on line seventeen."

Detective James Whittaker pulled his attention from the murder case file he was reviewing to stare at his squadmate. "My *what*?"

Arthur Freeman, Whittaker's usual partner in the Baltimore City Police Department, was leaning back in his chair, a grin on his wrinkled face. "Your wench. Those were her words."

Whittaker raised an eyebrow as he pressed the button for extension 2117. "Since when are you my wench?"

"Since it's Talk Like a Pirate Day, me hearty. Arrr!" Cassie Ellis said, then stifled a giggle.

He shook his head. "Talk Like a Pirate Day?"

"Aye. 'Tis every September 19th. Quit rolling yer eyes," she said in a firm tone that stopped him mid-roll. "It's a real—I mean, 'tis a real holiday. Fer over ten years now."

He moved the manila folder he had been reading in order to see his desk calendar. "Ah…so how does one celebrate Talk Like a Pirate Day?"

"By talkin' like a pirate, of course, matey. Have you hanged anyone from the yardarm? Killed any bilge-sucking rapscallions with your cutlass?"

Whittaker glanced down at his Glock, the closest thing he had to a cutlass. "Not lately." When he heard Cassie sigh, he added a half-hearted, "Arrrr."

"Oh, that sounded *real* enthusiastic, James. Anyway, I was wondering if you wanted to come over tonight and…shiver me timbers."

He laughed. "Now *that* I can be enthusiastic about. But I don't get off work until after eleven tonight." Glancing at the right corner of his computer, he noted there were six hours to go. The first quarter of his shift had been rather quiet. He hoped the rest of the night would be the same.

"No problem, me matey. Actually, after you sailed out of port last night, I got inspired and wrote in me logbook for three hours. Okay, let me talk normal for a bit. Since I wrote until 4 a.m., I slept late this morning. Thank God for the automatic cat feeder or Donner would have woken me up much earlier."

Donner meowed in the background at the mention of his name. Whittaker enjoyed picturing them. Cassie in the kitchen, where she spent the majority of her time; Donner near the food bowl, where he spent the majority of his time. In honor of the holiday, Whittaker added an eye patch to the cat and a wench costume to Cassie in his imaginary scene. With her red curls and blue eyes, she'd look fantastic. He had to clear his suddenly dry throat slightly before speaking. "Well, if you don't mind me getting there late, I'll come over after shift change." There were definitely advantages to dating an author.

"I'll even feed you. I've got some pirate grub for ye, also known as jambalaya."

"I'll be there, then. As long as we don't get a call. I'm next up." He winced as the other line lit up. Freeman picked it up before it could do more than bleep. Whittaker eyed his partner, heart sinking when the older man nodded toward him, then jerked his head slightly in a we've-got-to-go motion.

"I spoke too soon," he told Cassie.

"You should have knocked on wood. Or a peg leg," she said. "Hopefully, you'll have an easy case to close. Call me if you'll be later than midnight. If not, just come over after you clap the dirty scallywag in irons and put him in the brig."

He rolled his eyes at her pirate lingo. Crazy woman.

* * * *

Cassie wasn't the only crazy one, Whittaker realized as he stepped out of his unmarked sedan onto the cobblestone pavement of Thames Street. All around him, people wearing eye patches, puffy shirts, and bandanas on their heads were stumbling about Fells Point, one of Baltimore's prime entertainment districts. Whittaker even saw several people with parrots on their shoulders.

He noticed that the crowd, even drunk, instantly recognized him and Freeman as cops. Word on the street was that whenever a black man and white man, wearing suits, were seen together, they were either police detectives, feds, or someone was filming the next *Men In Black* installment.

"Okay, so there's Captain Jack Sparrow," Freeman said as they approached the cordoned-off crime scene, where two actors playing dueling pirates had reportedly fought to the death, literally, an hour before, when the loser fell into the harbor.

Whittaker followed Freeman's gaze and had to agree that the distraught man talking to the uniform did look like Johnny Depp's character in *Pirates of the Caribbean.* He sported the complete ensemble: beaded dreadlocks, black-lined eyes, pale skin, trimmed mustache and goatee, and pirate clothing. "So does the guy who drowned look like whatshisname…Orlando Bloom's character?"

"Will Turner," Freeman answered. "And I guess we'll find out when the recovery divers bring him back up. Probably won't look too good, though."

Whittaker scanned the scene until he spotted the dive team. The waters of Baltimore's Inner Harbor offered poor visibility, so one diver on the surface was serving as tender, holding a rope to guide the virtually blind diver at the bottom. Whittaker saw the line go taut three times. Evidently the diver below had found something. Or someone.

He approached the Captain Sparrow lookalike and signaled the officer who had been speaking to him to step back. "I'm sorry to intrude. I'm Detective Whittaker." He pointed at his partner. "Detective Freeman."

The pirate-costumed man took a deep breath. "Shaun Gilmore."

"Can you tell me what happened?" Whittaker asked.

Gilmore looked back at the dark water. "It was crazy. I don't know what Larry was thinking. We were dueling, like we always do." He gestured toward the cutlass tucked in his belt. "We do it all the time, at Renaissance festivals, the Fells Point Fun Festival, SCA events." Whittaker raised his eyebrows. "SCA, that's the Society for Creative Anachronism. Basically, we've performed this duel everywhere. Larry's never done anything like this before."

"Larry?"

"Larry Bailey. We're business partners." Gilmore reached inside his doublet and pulled out a card.

Whittaker glanced down and did his best not to groan. The card read *Swashbucklers Arrrr Us.*

"So what exactly did Larry do today that he hasn't done before?" Whittaker angled his body to block Gilmore's view of the recovery divers pulling up the body.

He didn't move quickly enough. The pirate's already pale skin went dead white. Whittaker grasped Gilmore's shoulders and turned him around so his back was toward the water.

"What did he do, Mr. Gilmore?"

"Well, we've choreographed the duel so that Larry loses his cutlass and puts his hands up in surrender. Typically, then I force him to his knees, walk behind him, and pretend to knock him out."

"Okay." Whittaker did his best to focus on Gilmore's words and not the pirate hat.

"This time, we had a good crowd watching. And when I disarmed him, he turned to me and said, 'Well, you won. I guess I need to walk the plank.' And then he freaking jumped off the pier and into the water. I tried to grab him and stop him, but it was too late. With all the heavy garb on, he sank like a stone. I kept waiting for him to come up, but he didn't."

"Wouldn't he have realized the costume would weigh him down?" Whittaker asked after exchanging a dubious glance with Freeman. They had observed many examples of stupidity in past investigations, but this might be the worst.

"I would've thought so. Then again, he did have a lot of rum this evening." Gilmore glanced toward one of the many bars on the waterfront. He shuddered once, violently.

"Why didn't you go in after him?"

Gilmore shook his head. "I know how heavy our stuff is. If I had gone in, I would have gone under, too. And I'm not a good swimmer. I tried to get people to rescue him, and a few jumped in, but no one could find him."

Whittaker wasn't surprised. If Bailey had sunk to the bottom, it was way too far down for anyone to reach him. Huge sailing and freighter ships routinely docked at that pier, so obviously the water was quite deep.

"Were you paid to perform tonight?" Whittaker watched as the EMTs loaded the body bag into the ambulance.

"Yeah."

Shouldn't he have said *aye*? "By whom?"

"The Fells Point Foundation. They try to bring business here, so we were hired as entertainment. We're one of the best-known pirate-impersonator companies in the area."

"You do look like Captain Jack Sparrow," Freeman said, breaking in for the first time.

Gilmore swiveled his head sharply and sneered. "I am *not* Captain Jack Sparrow. *Swashbucklers Arrrr Us* is a historically accurate organization. We use only authentic costumes, weapons, and phrases. We act out historical events, not movies or books. It's all serious. Other than the 'Arrrr' in our name, which we only agreed to because Maggie thought it was clever. Oh, God, Maggie!" Gilmore spun around toward the gawking crowd. "She took a break for dinner before all this started. She's probably done by now."

Whittaker noticed the uniforms struggling to hold back an attractive woman wearing a pirate wench costume. He raised an eyebrow at the miniscule amount of fabric. Good thing that this September evening in Baltimore was warm or she'd be freezing.

Whittaker hazarded a guess. "Is that Maggie?"

"Yeah. She's another partner and performer in Swashbucklers."

As soon as Whittaker gestured to the officers to release her, she raced over.

"What's going on? Why are the police here? Are you okay?" the young woman asked with a mixture of concern and confusion.

"I'm fine, it's just..." Gilmore sighed, ignored the other questions, and turned back to Whittaker. "This is Maggie Patrickson. She's my girlfriend."

Whittaker detected a certain defensive note to that declaration. "No need to worry, Mr. Gilmore. I seldom hit on witnesses."

When Freeman coughed the word "Cassie," Whittaker made a mental note to smack his partner later. Cassie was the reason he'd used the word *seldom* instead of *never*.

Gilmore's girlfriend turned to face Whittaker, tucking a strand of dark hair beneath her bandana. "You can hit on me all you want, Officer Gray Eyes."

"Detective," he corrected, watching Gilmore's jaw tighten. "I'm Detective Whittaker, this is Detective Freeman. We're with Homicide."

"Homicide!" she squeaked. She grabbed Gilmore's arm and looked around frantically. "Oh, God. Where's Larry?"

When Gilmore shot him a pleading look, Whittaker answered, "I'm sorry to inform you that there was an incident this evening during the performance. Mr. Bailey is dead. He apparently drowned in the harbor."

He watched as all the color leached out of her tanned skin and tears filled her eyes. "No! No. What happened?"

Whittaker eyed the weeping woman closely as Gilmore related what had occurred. When Gilmore explained that Bailey had said he'd "walk the plank" before jumping in, Whittaker saw confusion in her eyes before she covered her face with both hands and sobbed.

"Excuse us for a moment." Whittaker and Freeman left Gilmore to comfort his girlfriend and walked over to the uniforms. "What are the witnesses saying, Officer...Franklin?" Whittaker asked.

The officer stood up taller for his report. "We've spoken with all the witnesses who stayed after the incident. That was most of them, fortunately. We got here pretty quickly, and I think everyone still thought it was part of the act. They all state that the two men, Bailey and Gilmore, were performing a highly skilled, highly intricate duel with cutlasses and daggers, which took them very close to the edge of the pier. Suddenly,

Bailey appeared to jump toward the water. Gilmore grabbed at him, but apparently too late."

"Was anyone close enough to hear their dialogue during this duel?"

"Initially, yes." Franklin checked his notes. "Mostly it was just taunts and threats back and forth, some of which were funny enough to make the crowd laugh. But as they approached the edge, they apparently dropped their voices. One of the witnesses said what she could hear sounded more like stage directions, like 'take a step to the left,' 'watch out for the lamp post,' things of that nature."

"Which witness was that?"

The officer nodded toward two people wrapped in blankets and sitting on one of the benches. "The one on the left. She was the first to go in after the guy, too. Name's Denise Rush. Guy with her is her husband, Tom."

"I'll take the wife, you take the husband," Whittaker told Freeman.

They walked toward the witnesses, with Whittaker's shoes making clopping noises on the cobblestoned streets the whole way. When he reached Mrs. Rush, she raised her head, tears in her eyes. Whittaker introduced himself and led her a few yards down the pier so they weren't within hearing distance of anyone.

"I was a lifeguard," Rush said when they stopped. "I should've been able to get to him. Maybe if I had reacted sooner." She scrubbed at her face. "No, what am I saying? It wouldn't have mattered. He went down so fast. I dove down as far as I could, and don't think I was anywhere near him. Not that you could tell in such murky water."

Whittaker offered her what comfort he could. "It's very deep in that location. There was nothing you could have done differently."

She blinked away her tears. "Thank you, Detective."

"When did you jump in after Mr. Bailey?"

"Is that his name?" Rush said. "I didn't know his name. I just watched some guy die, and I didn't know his name." She stared at the water and took a deep breath before answering his original question. "As soon as he fell in, pretty much. That other guy started yelling and pointing so I looked down and saw that he hadn't surfaced. I dove in."

"Did you hear anything before Mr. Bailey entered the water?"

The witness looked up at him. "Like what?"

Whittaker didn't want to lead her to the answer, so he skirted around it. "Maybe something that indicated what was about to happen. What led up to Mr. Bailey entering the water?"

Rush pursed her mouth in consideration. "I didn't hear anything that showed he was about to do *that*. Like I told the other officer, it was a lot of under-the-breath type of stuff, more stage directions. I think the one guy, Bailey…" She paused for a deep breath. "Bailey said, 'step to the left. We're too close to the edge,' and then the other guy—"

"Gilmore," Whittaker supplied.

"Gilmore said something like 'don't worry, I'm being careful. Are you careful?' Then Bailey said 'always.' Gilmore said something else, but I didn't hear it. Then they stepped even closer to the edge and said a few other things. I couldn't hear any of that though."

"Was anyone else near enough to hear?"

Rush glanced back at the edge of the pier, then shook her head. "Other than my husband, no, I don't think so. They were swinging their cutlasses all over the place. One of them even took out a dagger. They were probably stage props, but they looked sharp and shiny enough. So people were giving them a pretty wide berth."

"Did you see the other performer with them? The female?" Whittaker said, following a sudden hunch.

She surprised him with a laugh. "Oh, trust me, I saw her. So did my husband. She's hard not to notice." Rush sobered quickly, staring down at her clenched hands. "But that was earlier in the day. They've been performing all over the place. I don't think she was around during that final show. In fact, I remember that while we were sitting here, after the officers told us to wait to talk to a detective, she walked out of the pub across the street, then ran over when she noticed the crowd."

Whittaker ran through it again, but Rush's story didn't change much. After reconnecting with Freeman, who didn't have anything new to add from Rush's husband, Whittaker headed back to talk to Maggie Patrickson. When he took her aside, Gilmore didn't look pleased.

"Ms. Patrickson, how long have you known Mr. Bailey and Mr. Gilmore?"

She rubbed her eyes before answering. "I've been going out with Shaun for two years now, I guess. We met at the local theater."

"And Mr. Bailey?"

She blinked back tears. "We met about a year ago when we did a performance of *Pirates of Penzance*. We formed Swashbucklers right after that."

"Is there anything you know about Mr. Bailey that would have caused you to expect tonight's actions?"

"No. God, no. I can't imagine what would make him do that. It's crazy. Larry wasn't crazy."

"Could he have been under the influence of alcohol?" He could tell that Patrickson certainly was. He could smell the rum from three feet away.

She shrugged. "I don't know. Maybe when he took his dinner break. We alternate so there are always at least two people performing. We take our jobs very seriously. Larry, especially. He was obsessed with accuracy, read up on real pirates, refused to participate in what he called 'pirate myths' like talking about buried treasure or singing 'Fifteen Men on a Dead Man's Chest' and stuff like that. He said that was all stuff from the movies."

Whittaker waved his hand up and down, indicating her costume. "This outfit is accurate?"

She glanced down. "This? Well, no." She tried to smile through the tears. "I used to dress up like a female pirate, but since that just meant I dressed like a man, it wasn't terribly popular with our audiences. People seemed to like this costume more…especially drunk frat boys. Our repeat business went up when I switched to this outfit. Neither guy liked it—Shaun since he'd get jealous and Larry due to the inaccuracy—but they had to admit the company was doing better with it."

"So you don't know what could have happened tonight?"

"No. He was happy. We were all happy."

* * * *

Whittaker and his partner talked to several more people, finishing up with Shaun Gilmore again. No one added anything important to their previous account. They notified Bailey's parents of his death—a task Whittaker would never grow used to—and now they were back in the office. Whittaker stared at the computer screen, reading up on *Swashbucklers*. The online reviews of the company were good—plenty of positive comments on Maggie Patrickson, especially. There were also several mentions of their authenticity and attention to detail.

There was no mention of any incidents or issues. No obvious money problems. No criminal records on any of the performers, other than several unpaid parking and speeding tickets for Patrickson. Nothing pointed toward foul play. Perhaps Freeman was right, and this was just a case of death by stupidity.

It wouldn't be the first time. Just last month, Whittaker and Freeman investigated a case in which the deceased had been found nude, with duct tape covering his entire head. It appeared to be homicide, but after a thorough and bizarre investigation, they found evidence that the deceased had unusual inclinations, including autoerotic asphyxiation. The idiot did it to himself. So it wasn't farfetched to speculate that Bailey decided to do this one trick to delight the crowd without considering that he was weighed down by heavy period clothing. It was like that Warner

Brothers cartoon, when Daffy blows himself up and says, “I can only do it once.”

Whittaker’s phone rang, and he cursed as he read Cassie’s number on the display. He’d forgotten to let her know he’d miss dinner. “Sorry, honey, I got tied up,” he said in lieu of a greeting.

“I hope not literally,” she said. “Did someone tie ye up to the mainmast?”

Good. Cassie obviously wasn’t mad at him, since she was still using pirate speak. “No, not literally. The only thing I’m tied to is the computer screen. Research.”

“So, who died?”

“A pirate.”

She took a moment to respond. “Seriously? What happened, did someone fire off a flintlock?”

“No. Accidental death, probably. We had some pirate re-enactors performing a choreographed duel, and then one of them ended up in the harbor. Not sure yet if he jumped in, fell in, or was pushed in. Regardless, he went straight down to Davey Jones’s locker.”

“Nice pirate reference, but, wow, that’s odd. Was alcohol involved? Or more to the point, too much rum?”

“Maybe.” He shrugged. “Anyway, sorry I’m going to miss dinner.”

“Have ye had any grub tonight?”

“No.” He looked down when his stomach grumbled. “Something my body just reminded me of.”

“I can bring you over some jambalaya, and we can eat there. Not the intimate dinner I planned, but it’ll work.”

“I’d love it. I’ll be the envy of the department, eating your food instead of takeout.” He grinned over at Freeman who was frowning at him over what looked like a ham sandwich.

“Since Freeman is probably scowling at you, tell him I’ll bring him some, too,” Cassie said. “Be there in ten minutes.”

Whittaker hung up, walked to Freeman’s desk, and leaned against it. “Throw that thing away.” He nodded at Freeman’s sandwich. “Cassie’s bringing over some real food. Pirate grub.”

“You’re spoiled.”

“I am.” Whittaker grinned. “Be happy I share. Cassie’s a great cook. But more amazing, she doesn’t get bent out of shape when I work late. I love her flexibility.”

Freeman snorted. “I’m sure you do.”

Whittaker smacked his partner on the back of the head. “Not that way.” He called down to the parking lot and let them know to expect a visitor. Then he went back to his research.

"Have you found anything about a life insurance policy?" Whittaker asked a couple minutes later. Bailey's parents had been too devastated when they were informed of their son's death to answer any questions about finances.

"Not according to his insurance agent," Freeman said, lifting up the evidence bag that contained Bailey's soggy belongings. Freeman's first job had been to call up the local agent they had found listed in Bailey's wallet.

Whittaker went back to researching the company. When Cassie called him from her car, he took the elevator down to the garage level and escorted her back up to the fifth floor. "So how was your day?" he asked, enjoying the smell wafting from the bag he'd taken from her. "Did you get some writing done?"

"Some. Mostly I did research." As they stepped off the elevator, she perused the pictures of wanted criminals hanging on the bulletin boards. "Nope, still don't recognize anyone."

"What did you research? Something for your latest book?"

"Pirates, actually." She pushed open the door to the homicide department and called out greetings to the detectives she knew. "It's fascinating stuff."

"If you say so." They reached Whittaker's desk. He pulled the containers from the bag. "You thinking of making your next book *The Marauder Murders* to stay with your 'M' alliteration theme?"

"No," Cassie said as she portioned out the food. "I just got distracted."

After Freeman grabbed his plate with a smile and returned to his desk, Whittaker settled behind his own. He scooped up some jambalaya, enjoying the spicy blend of chicken, sausage, and rice. "I'm rather sick of pirates, to tell the truth. Fells Point was crazy."

"I'm sure." Cassie pulled a chair to Whittaker's desk. "But those aren't *real* pirates. That's just people imitating what they see in movies. It's not accurate. For example, I read that there were only three instances when pirates buried their treasure. And they never needed maps to find it again, since it was evidently so poorly hidden, it was immediately found."

Whittaker continued to eat his dinner as he listened to Cassie spout off facts about pirates. It fascinated him how much she enjoyed her research, regardless of the subject. She would talk with the same gusto about decaying corpses, effects of poisons, or the history of the Baltimore Orioles.

"And then there's the ridiculous idea of parley. Like pirates are really going to let a prisoner have temporary protection until they work out a negotiation. Pirates didn't do that. Sure, they had some code of ethics, but that was more to maintain order on a ship. They truly were ruthless, at least some of them at…"

He tuned out for a while, enjoying the sound of her voice but thinking about today's case. There was something wrong. He didn't trust Gilmore…or Maggie Patrickson. At the very least, he wouldn't trust her if he were dating her. She had checked him out a little too easily for his liking, especially while standing next to her boyfriend of two years.

Of course, infidelity doesn't make for a murderer. Plus, she wasn't on the scene when the death occurred so how—

He tuned back into Cassie's conversation. "What did you just say?"

She and Freeman were laughing, most likely at him. "I said it was true that pirates carried pterodactyls on their shoulders. I wanted to see if you were paying attention."

"Ha-ha. I was paying attention, mostly." He was relieved that she didn't seem annoyed at him. Since she often spaced out into her own thoughts and plotting, she never complained when he did the same. Another advantage to dating an author. "So is the parrot thing true?"

"Actually, that does look to be true. Pirates traveled to exotic places, and parrots were easy to take care of. Plus they'd fetch a good price at various ports. But another thing that isn't true is…"

Piracy was often about money and greed, Whittaker mused, tuning into his own thoughts again. Could greed have played a role in this drowning? It did in many homicides, but he couldn't see how it related to this death. According to the *Swashbucklers Arrrr Us* website, the team had appeared at many locations, so they were busy. But they didn't charge much per gig. So probably no one would gain financially from Bailey's death. And again, it looked like an accident. Was he suspicious for no reason or—

"What did you say?" This time he was drawn back into Cassie's monologue for a different reason.

"I said that the whole 'walking the plank' thing was a fabrication as well. It was easier to just toss them over the side, or abandon them to starve on a deserted island, or if you were in a bad mood, keelhaul them. But 'walk the plank' was more a fabrication of fiction books."

Whittaker stared over at Freeman. They both dropped their spoons and stood up. "Hey, Garcia," Whittaker called to a detective a few desks over. "Can you walk Cassie out?"

"Aye aye, captain," he answered.

Whittaker leaned over and kissed Cassie on the nose. "You've just given us a lead. I'll see you later tonight."

* * * *

Yes, there were definitely advantages to having an author as a girlfriend.

Armed with Cassie's info that walking the plank was a myth, Whittaker brought Gilmore in for interrogation. It didn't take long to get the truth out of the young man, especially after Freeman pushed the medical examiner for Bailey's blood alcohol content. It was only .01, far too low to have affected Bailey's thought processes, and far, far too low for Gilmore's story that Bailey had been drinking a lot to be true. After Whittaker pointed out Gilmore's lies, as well as the shallow dagger wound that the M.E. had found on the body, Gilmore confessed quickly.

Although it was late by the time Whittaker finished booking Gilmore, he headed to Cassie's to thank her for her information. He filled her in on the case as she got them both drinks.

"Well, I'm glad you were paying attention to me, James. And it's cool that I helped you close a case."

"You definitely did." He sat down on the couch and slipped out of his shoes, laughing when the cat came over to bury his face in the smelly interior of one of his loafers. "It seemed unlikely that someone as obsessed with accuracy as the victim would ever turn around and talk about 'walking the plank.' Gilmore made that part up. Evidently what they were really saying under their breath was about Patrickson. Gilmore had told Bailey that it wasn't careful to leave his sweatshirt in Maggie's bedroom."

"Ah, so cheating rears its ugly head," Cassie said.

"You got it. The victim and Patrickson had evidently been having an affair for months. So Gilmore decided to get rid of his competition. He also had a real dagger with him for this fight instead of a prop."

"So that's why Bailey jumped away."

"Correct. In fact, we found a small wound on the right side of his body, along with a hole in his doublet. So Gilmore did get a slight poke in, just enough to let his former friend know he was serious."

"Then Gilmore pretended to try and grab him?" Cassie asked. "Pretty ballsy move to kill someone in front of an audience."

"Agreed." He leaned down to scratch Donner, who had draped his dark, furry body over both shoes. "He said he thought it would convince everyone that it had been Bailey's stupidity that led to his death. Initially, he had decided to have an 'accident' during a duel practice, then decided it would be more effective in front of people. Anyway, thank you again for your help." He kissed her.

"My pleasure. Now, maybe you can help me." She nestled against him and ran her fingers through his hair. "I've been writing a love scene, and I'm afraid I'm suffering from writer's block. How about we re-enact it and see if you can provide some inspiration?"

Oh yeah, there were definitely advantages to dating an author.

Cathy Wiley is happiest when plotting stories in her head or on the computer, or when she's delving into research. She draws upon her experience in the hospitality business to show the lighter, quirkier side of people and upon her own morbid mind to show the darker side.

In her free time, she enjoys scuba diving, dancing, wine, food, and reading. She lives outside of Baltimore, Maryland, with two very spoiled cats. www.cathywiley.com

HALLOWEEN

PREMONITION

by Art Taylor

In the dream, you wander down an endless hallway in a loose nightgown, glancing in door after door, looking for something, looking *out* for something. Or someone. Your hand clutches a slip of paper, so tightly that your fingernails cut your palm, and on the paper, you can make out a string of blotted numbers.

With a start, you open your eyes and see the clock flash out the time, 2:43 a.m., but you don't hesitate. You throw back the covers of your bed and scramble up to sit on your pillow, the nightgown bunching at your hips. You flick on the light, you grab the phone, you dial the numbers from your dream carefully, one digit at a time. You have indeed been clenching your fist in your sleep, a nail has broken, and the indentations in your palm shine fiery red—blood? No, no, just flecks of polish. Your breath, heavy and wild at the first ring, deepens with the second and the third. *Just a dream*, you think after the fourth ring has steadied your panting, and you start to hang up. *After all, what should I say to...whoever answers? A nightmare—something terrible—worry, fear, panic....* Then: *Overreaction. Stupidity.* But before you can replace the receiver, you hear a scrambling on the other end of the line. With another glimpse at the clock—2:45—you ready your apology.

"Oh, help me, help me," comes a weak voice, struggling and desperate. "Oh, please, whoever you are, wherever you are, he's—" and the line goes dead.

A cold terror cuts up your spine. Your thoughts race frantically, but your body, for the moment, is paralyzed. Your hand trembles as you struggle to get a new dial tone, and you fumble twice before hitting the right keys.

"9-1-1, what's your—"

"Oh, please help," you cry. "I've had a nightmare and when I woke—"

With a start—

You wake.

The covers of the bed are still pulled tight against your chin. The lights of the room are still off. On your nightstand, the clock shows 1:28, and by the glowing redness of those numbers, you see the edges of your phone, the receiver still in place. Thin moonbeams pierce through the gap between your curtains, and your cat, curled into a ball at the end of your bed, stretches in the dappled glow. Something about her calms you. Your breath steadies. Your pulse slows. You glance around the rest of the room to see the reflection of the moonlight in the mirror over your dresser and, in the corner, the outline of your chair.

And suddenly your breath is gone again.

Someone's sitting there—watching you. Waiting.

You see his pale arm in the moonlight, then the shadow of his other arm hanging motionless from a thin torso. *Him.*

You barely manage to keep yourself from crying out. You wonder if you can grab the baseball bat just on the other side of your nightstand. You wish you'd taken your father's advice and gotten a gun. Then you remember the blouse you'd laid out for tomorrow. As your eyes focus, the wooziness of sleep finally falling away, you realize that's all it is, hanging limp across the back of the chair.

Overreaction. Stupidity. Your nerves are just on edge. The nightmare, the darkness…and this night itself, of course. Halloween, for Christ's sake. That parade of ghosts and ghouls darting door to door earlier in the evening had gotten to you. And nothing but horror movies on the TV before you went to bed. A chill wind has been rustling and scattering the leaves all night. And then there's that moon looming above the oaks in the yard.

But you'd thought *him.*

And who *was* the him you thought might be sitting there watching you?

Your brother maybe? Drunk again, and stopping by after the bars just to chat, passing out in your chair? It's happened before. Or your ex-boyfriend, still carrying the torch, persistent with his calls and emails and now pushing the boundaries a step too far? You'd always wondered if he'd made a duplicate key. Or were you thinking of…

Somewhere in the distance you hear laughter—more than one person. This laughter, you know, is real. But you can't gauge the direction or the distance. Not yet.

Layers of darkness shroud the other side of the room, but you know the door of the closet and the door to the hallway stand closed. Easing back the edge of the covers, you reach up to turn on the lamp. Your cat wakes when the light floods the room. It blinks its eyes and stretches. You rise and, still gaining your balance, find your way across the carpet, picking up that baseball bat and pushing that white shirt down into a ball on the chair. Surely there's nothing behind either door—you *know* this, the laughter wasn't *that* close—but you go through the motions anyway. Which one to open first? You decide on the closet, raise the bat high, and with a deep breath, fling open the door.

No one jumps out. Of course.

And there's no one hiding in the hallway either.

And as you work your way through the house—checking behind the shower curtain and in the hot water heater closet, in the laundry room and the second bedroom—you began to ease your grip on the bat. The front door is still bolted shut, and the second latch remains in place. The door to the patio is locked, and when you glance through vertical blinds, you find the plastic chairs and table as empty as always in that same moonlight.

And there, just beyond, you find the source of the laughter: the dregs of your neighbor's Halloween party, the one he'd invited you to—a courtesy, you know (an invitation you'd just as courteously declined). A keg sits in the center of his deck, and he's got his feet propped up on it, leaning back on his own plastic chair. Only two others with him, at least two that you can see—two men, one dressed as a pirate, the other a gangster. You see the latter's tommy gun resting on the railing. Wind chimes clink and jingle, a murmur of conversation, more laughter—just a little too loud, after just a little too much to drink. You know how those parties go. Your neighbor himself is in some sort of skeleton costume, a black outfit with white bones, faintly glowing. The thin bones of his forearm rest motionless on the arm of his chair.

And then you see that he's seen you. That he's looking your way.

Quickly, you pull the blinds tight again, press your hands against them to keep them from swinging, look down at what you're wearing—just that thin nightgown, barely hanging to your knees.

The conversation out there, the laughter that you'd heard, stops.

You wait. You don't hear anything more from over there, nothing but those wind chimes, and that same rustle of leaves through the small yard that separates your house from his…because he's just told them to keep it down, right?…because *you've* told him to keep it down before. More than once. The houses aren't so far apart, and the noise carries, and you've tried to smile each time you've explained this to him and tried to accept his own smile as genuine, even though you've felt his impatience, those little hints of disdain. Entitlement, arrogance. Something cold in those eyes, too—something you saw the very first time you met him, when he asked if you were seeing anyone, asked why you weren't, asked if there was any chance.... Something cold in those eyes when you'd politely declined his interest, something lifeless there.

Those same eyes that just caught you looking at him through the blinds.

You wait. You hear nothing.

When you peek through the window again, the pirate and the gangster have disappeared. The skeleton sits alone, openly staring at your house now. As you watch, he tips back his beer, almost like he's sending a toast your way.

You shut the blinds quickly.

You promise yourself not to dare another look.

When you return to your room, you lay the bat beside you on the bed. It is exactly 2:01 when you pull the covers up to your chin, 2:04 when you look down to find your cat curling up once more into a ball at your feet, and by 2:15 you've successfully resisted the urge to call someone. And who would you call anyway? That brother of yours, long since deep in his Halloween drink and helpless himself? That ex-boyfriend, a mistake in the first place and one you don't need to compound? Your father, asleep himself, and two states away?

Overreaction.... Stupidity. Of course.

And Halloween, you think again. The spirit of the season. Just something in the air.

But you find yourself unable to sleep. The wind has picked up now, you can hear it in the swish and whisper of those leaves, and in those wind chimes, too, like change in a stranger's pocket. The refrigerator has never seemed to hum so loudly, and the ice falling into its bin sounds like glass breaking somewhere close by. Something in the hallway creaks. You tell yourself it's always made that sound.

But the worst of it isn't the noise at all. It's the clock's calm measure of minutes and the waiting silence of the phone.

You watch them both without blinking, fearful despite yourself of what might happen just before the time comes and the phone rings.

Because the phone number in the dream had, of course, been your own.

Art Taylor's fiction has appeared in anthologies including *Chesapeake Crimes: This Job Is Murder* and *The Crooked Road, Volume 3*, and in *Ellery Queen's Mystery Magazine*. "When Duty Calls," his story for the previous Chesapeake Crimes anthology, won him a third Derringer Award and was a finalist for the Agatha and the Macavity. "The Care and Feeding of Houseplants" (*EQMM*) won the Agatha in 2014. An assistant professor at George Mason University, he reviews crime fiction for the *Washington Post*. www.arttaylorwriter.com.

DISCO DONNA

by Shari Randall

"Hippies?"

"It's a Halloween costume emergency," I said.

Mrs. Maven nodded and pushed her way through racks of vintage clothes. I figured if anyone could help Berks find a costume at the last minute, it would be Mrs. Maven.

Eunice and I had our bell bottoms and flower power ready to go. Berks, however, complained that hip huggers hugged her big hips too hard. She had a point. She's definitely curvy.

"Not much in here," Mrs. Maven said.

She owns the storefront on Elm Street that houses both Roseport Retro Rags and Cookie's Bakery. There isn't much else in Roseport. It's a bucolic village, or at least that's what it says in the real-estate brochures. Cookie's is the place where everyone meets, and Retro is where high-school kids shop for cool stuff. Since Mrs. Maven is the world's biggest gossip, she keeps the door between the two shops open, so occasionally you'll see teachers from the high school come in for coffee and pastry, which is awkward for kids like us if we've just skipped school. Aside from that, though, the combo is heaven. Pastry and vintage clothes: two of my favorite things.

"Just got a box of new stuff in. Some of it looks hippyish to me." She waved at a box on the counter. "Came from the people who bought that rundown Victorian on the edge of Hamilton Park. They're living with friends while they gut it. They found some boxes in a crawl space." She opened the cardboard box. "They took a box of books to the library book sale and brought the clothes here. Fortunately, the attic was dry. Doesn't look like any mice got at it. Help yourselves." She waved a vague peace sign and left us with the box.

Berks and I dug in, giggling at the headbands, tie-dye shirts, and patchwork skirts, draping ourselves with macramé necklaces and beads, and posing in front of a cloudy floor-length mirror making peace signs.

"Some of these clothes are a bit more seventies," I said. I held up a pair of Frye boots and hot pants. "Not so much hippie. Kind of disco."

Berks tugged a polyester halter dress over her jeans and T-shirt, pulled up her curly black hair, and twirled. "Very *Saturday Night Fever*, don't you think?"

Berks danced over to Cookie's door, waved to Mrs. Maven, then danced back. I shook my head. Berks had a very big comfort zone. I shrugged into another silky dress but it hung slack on me. Curvy I'm not.

"That dress works for you, Berks," I noted. "You're about the size of whoever owned these clothes."

"Maybe you could wear this skirt." Berks tossed a denim mini to me, then perched some pot-leaf sunglasses on my nose.

I frowned. "Too short. My mom would never let me out of the house in this. Cool patch pockets, though."

I put my hand into one of the pockets and pulled out a crumpled piece of paper. "Hey, what's this?" I smoothed it out on my knee. "It's a study hall pass from Roseport High! 'Please excuse Donna Demonte from gym class.'"

Berks's face clouded. "Oh, my God. Donna Demonte."

"Who?" I tossed the skirt back in the box.

"You don't know Disco Donna?" Berks shrieked and clawed at her dress. "Eew! Disco Donna! I'm wearing a dead girl's dress!" She stumbled backward into a mannequin, sending it tumbling to the floor.

"Oh, my God! *The* Disco Donna!"

The commotion drew Mrs. Maven. "Girls! What is it?"

"Mrs. Maven, do you remember that high-school girl who was killed? Disco, er, Donna Demonte?" I handed her the hall pass.

Mrs. Maven's eyes widened as she studied the paper. "How could I forget? That poor girl was murdered."

Mrs. Maven and I helped Berks pick the mannequin up off the floor. We peeled the dress off Berks, while she continued to shudder and moan. Several customers from Cookie's Bakery had poked their heads in to see what the commotion was about. In the crowd, I saw the very disapproving face of our high-school principal. Time to go!

We thanked Mrs. Maven and hustled from the shop as quickly as possible, leaving Mrs. Maven to share this delicious nugget of news with the folks at Cookie's.

"I cannot believe I touched a dead girl's stuff." Berks passed me a mini bottle of hand sanitizer as we hustled to our volunteer gig at the Roseport Library. Her mom makes her take sanitizer everywhere. "You wore a dead girl's glasses, too."

“Eeew,” I shrieked, then started giggling. Nerves, probably, but it was kind of exciting in a way. Some towns had haunted houses, or a ghostly black dog, or the Bunny Man who killed partying teens. We had Disco Donna, our unsolved crime, our urban legend.

Donna had been queen bee of Roseport High back in the seventies. Head cheerleader, bad rep, too hot to care. The morning after Halloween, she was found laid out on her bed real peaceful, with a red rose in her clasped hands, bruises around her neck. People said a madman had escaped from the sanitarium in Springfield and climbed in her window and strangled her. Or it was the head football player or the president of the student council. Everyone had a theory. People whispered. They said her mom went mental when she found her and left her room unchanged like a shrine for years. If a girl told the story, they always mentioned the rose. If a boy told the story, they always said she was naked.

Her killer was never found.

“You know what?” Berks gave me the one-eyebrow-raised smirk that was a sure sign that she was about to make a bad decision. “That dress would make an awesome costume!” She spun on her heel. “I’m going to buy it. It fit me perfectly. I am going to be Disco Donna for Halloween tonight!”

“That is a monumentally gross idea,” I said. “What if the dress is haunted?”

Berks shrieked with laughter and told me she’d catch up with me later.

I ran up the steps of the Roseport Library, a pretty stone building on the edge of Hamilton Park. The library was the other town hub, so I didn’t mind volunteering there. The librarians were nice, with one exception. Mrs. Davis Keen, The Dragon Queen. She could make a table of teen delinquents pack up and leave with just a single death-ray glance, so when she was there we were on our best behavior.

I waved to Mrs. Day, the cool children’s librarian, and hurried into the staff-only area to get a book cart, praying that Mrs. Davis Keen wouldn’t notice that Berks was late. A half hour later, Berks dashed in, face flushed, holding her bag with The Dress. We hurried into the staff room. Tillie Thompson, a tiny older lady, was there sorting through some boxes. I stopped short.

“Remember what Mrs. Maven said?” I whispered. “She said the people who brought in the clothes also dropped a box of books at the library.”

“Oh, my God, oh, my God,” Berks whispered hoarsely, grabbing my arm. “Dead girl’s books!”

Mrs. Thompson reached into a canvas bin so deep that her toes barely touched the floor. "Need some help?" I asked.

"You girls are the best." Mrs. Thompson smiled. "We got a lot of boxes today. I've got to run, but if you can just get them on the table, I can sort through them tomorrow. Could you finish up for me?"

Could we ever. As Mrs. Thompson twinkled out, we took the remaining three boxes of books from the bin.

Keeping an eye peeled for the Dragon Queen, we rooted quickly through the boxes. One box held paperback romances. Cover after cover trimmed in pink, with shirtless men and half-naked women clinging to them. We rolled our eyes and moved on to the next box. Ludlum, Benchley, Jacqueline Suzanne. That left one box. It almost vibrated with—what? It was just an old cardboard box, but my hands shook as I pulled the flaps open, and I could tell Berks was holding her breath.

High-school textbooks. Very old high-school textbooks. *Earth Science. Algebra and You*. "Oh, no!" I gasped. "Should we be wearing gloves?" We were huge fans of *CSI*.

"Her killer probably didn't handle her textbooks, unless he was a complete weirdo," Berks said.

I unfolded a poster of a skinny, bare-chested rock singer with amazing blond hair. Frampton Comes Alive.

"Kind of hot," Berks said. She put it back in the box. "Look! A Roseport yearbook."

We flipped it open and thumbed through the pages. "Oh, my God, look at those glasses! And those prom pictures. Ruffles!"

The intercom squawked. "Mrs. Davis Keen? Back room phone."

"Quick!" Berks grabbed her shopping bag and thrust the yearbook inside. "Let's put the other books back in the box and get this later."

My hands shook as I hurried to replace the textbooks in the box. In my haste, I knocked the huge algebra book off the table. It fell open. We gasped.

The pages had been glued together, then hollowed out. Tucked in the hollow was a pink notebook.

I pulled it out. On the cover, someone had written in purple looping handwriting: *Diary*. I felt like it was burning my hand as I pushed it into the shopping bag, too. Berks shoved the bag onto a shelf just as Mrs. Davis Keen entered the room.

"Hi Mrs. Dra— er, Mrs. Davis Keen. We were just helping Mrs. Thompson with those donations," I stammered.

Mrs. Davis Keen swept her laser beams over us but evidently was too busy thinking about important library business to detect our nervous energy. "Thank you, girls. I'm sure she appreciates it."

She lifted the phone, listened for a few seconds, and said, "There are some new boxes here. I'll check them now."

She powered over to the boxes we had rifled. "These came in today?"

"Um, I think that's what Mrs. Thompson said." We edged toward the door.

"Move along, girls. Get back to your shelving," she murmured as her beautifully manicured hands lifted the flaps on one of the cartons.

We pushed our book carts into the children's room. "Why is she going through those boxes? She never looks at donations," I whispered.

When Mrs. Day, the children's librarian, popped around the corner, I almost died.

"She's there because someone told her the books were donated by the people who bought the old Demonte house," she said. "You know how people are. If anyone hears that we have books from Disco Donna's house, they'll cause a disturbance. And you know how Mrs. D-K feels about disturbances."

We finished our shift and hurried to the back room as casually as possible and grabbed Berks's shopping bag. When we ran out, I was certain that the bag was glowing radioactively and we had "Stealing Disco Donna's Diary" in a huge thought bubble over our heads.

We hurried to my house. I texted our friend Eunice. She had to see the diary and yearbook A.S.A.P.

Berks and I sat in my room staring at the plastic bag, which sat on the floor in the corner. It seemed to breathe. I did not want it on my bed. I was dying to look at it but knew that Eunice would kill if she learned Berks and I had gone ahead without her.

I heard Eunice's mom's van wheeze to a stop in front of the house, and then the sound of footsteps as Eunice pounded up the stairs.

"What's this all about?" Eunice exclaimed. She was wearing a perfectly coordinated hippie outfit, including a purple pimp-like hat. "What's this about Disco Donna?"

"Shhhh!" I grabbed her arm and pointed at the bag.

"Disco Donna's shopping bag?" Eunice deadpanned.

We dissolved into shrieks of laughter, but I shushed everyone again. "This is for real," I said.

"Really real," Berks whispered.

I filled Eunice in.

Our eyes turned again to the bag. Berks grabbed it, and we flung ourselves on the floor.

We went through the yearbook first, flipping to the D's. "That's her," I whispered.

Donna looked out at us with dark, almond-shaped eyes ringed with heavy eyeliner. She wore huge hoop earrings. A mane of dark curls. Her smile was flirtatious, almost a smirk.

"She kind of looks like you, Berks," Eunice whispered.

Berks snorted. "Maybe she looks like me with way too much makeup and attitude. Supposedly she was pretty slutty, right? That's not me."

Eunice flipped open the diary. "Look, she dots her I's with bubbly hearts. My auntie says that means you're weak minded."

"She doesn't look weak to me," I said.

I could hear my mom answer the doorbell downstairs, but the voices of little kids yelling "trick or treat" faded into the background as Eunice read the diary entries. Donna noted big events, which sounded pretty wild. Fights with her mom, whom she called a "slut," "fat pig," and "jailer." Donna never mentioned girl friends, but she had a lot of boyfriends. Occasionally she'd doodle hearts, flowers, and peace signs, and after most entries she'd write "Keep my secrets safe, Peter! SWAK." Page after page describing make-outs with Jimmy, Paulie Sugarboy, Billy, Chris, Scott the Hickey King, and some nameless boy she did IT with in the janitor's closet after a basketball game. We were riveted. September of her junior year, she started mentioning Mr. X.

"Dear Diary, I'm calling him Mr. X because if that Fat Pig sees this, we'll get in trouble. Mr. X is an older man. So much more mature than those high school boys. A REAL Man. He says I'm his Special Lady. I can't wait to see him Saturday. I'll have lots to tell you when I get back!" Hearts, hearts, hearts.

"He climbed the trellis last night. He said it was time to make me HIS WOMAN. He touched my dirty word with his dirty word and then he dirty word dirty word dirty word," Eunice read.

"Give me that!" Berks snatched the diary from Eunice's hands and began to read.

In October, things had changed. A few pages were ripped to shreds, evidently by Donna digging in with her pen.

"Dear Diary: It's REALLY REALLY true. How could he do this to me? He said we'd leave together and move away and he'd get a job in another school."

"Another school? He was old enough to work in her school?" Eunice gasped.

"A teacher? That's gross!" I shuddered.

"Creep." Berks flipped the page.

"Cindy Pertaki. Why her? She's a total slut. She thinks she's hot stuff with that Camaro. How could he do that? Why!!!!! If he won't leave her, I will tell. EVERYONE. Because he promised we'd be together. Forever."

"That's the last entry," Berks said, leafing forward through some blank pages just to make sure.

I grabbed the yearbook and pawed through it until I found a picture of Cindy Pertaki. A blonde with soft eyes and a lot of cleavage stared soulfully at us.

"That's the sophomore section," Berks said. "Mr. X was a cradle robber."

"The last entry was two days before Halloween," I noted. "And Disco Donna died on Halloween."

Eunice stared. "So that means—"

Berks looked at us. "What? What does it mean?"

"Mr. X had to hide his games with his students. When Donna threatened to tell on him—"

"He had to shut her up," Eunice finished my sentence.

Berks whispered, "Mr. X killed Disco Donna."

We were quiet for awhile. Eunice twirled her hair. Berks bit her fingernails. I flipped through the yearbook to the teachers' pages.

Row upon row of serious-looking men and women stared out, black and white pictures of respectable, middle-aged educators. Berks stabbed a photo of a blond man with aviator glasses. "There. The gym teacher. They're always so full of themselves."

We contemplated the gym teacher, Cale Smith.

"He's not my type," Eunice declared.

"Mine either." Berks turned the book, squinted. "He looks a little like our Principal Smith, doesn't he? If Principal Smith were a lot more handsome and had hair? I wonder if that's him."

"Doesn't matter about our types, it had to be Disco Donna's type." I flipped back to the student section.

Berks gasped. "Wait! That's, that's—" she jabbed the page. "My uncle Paul. Paul Sugarman."

A skinny boy with long black hair, braces, and a mangy moustache grinned from the page. Everyone knew Berks's uncle. He was on the town police force. Now he weighed twice as much and had half as much hair as the boy in the picture. Thankfully, he no longer had a moustache.

"Your uncle was Paulie Sugarboy?" I started giggling. Berks blushed.

"Well, this probably means that your uncle is a psycho killer, Berks," Eunice said. "Even though he seems pretty nice now. Maybe it was a crime of jealous passion."

Berks shot Eunice a killer look.

"Wait, wait," I said. "You're forgetting. Disco Donna practically points the finger at Mr. X. Seems like she and Paulie, er, Uncle Paul, whatever, were just a passing thing. It was probably a teacher."

It was hard to see what any teenage girl would see in these guys, since the clothes and glasses and hairstyles were so unflattering. We flipped through, muttering "How about him?" but didn't get killer vibes from anyone other than the chemistry teacher, who looked like he'd spent way too much time with the formaldehyde.

"We should call the police. We have new information that could crack the case," Eunice said.

"Correction. We *stole* information that could crack the case," Berks said.

"We didn't know it was Donna's. Oh wait, we did," I said.

We paced, bit our nails, twirled our hair, and avoided each other's eyes.

"Wait a minute." I flipped through the diary. "She keeps mentioning this guy Peter who keeps her secrets safe. Maybe he knew."

"What if Peter was the killer?" Eunice's eyes glowed. "Peter gets to hear from this hot girl about other men, but secretly he's in love with her? It might drive him wild with jealousy."

"That's a good theory. I saw a movie like that on Lifetime," Berks said.

"But the timing," I said. "This Peter has heard about all these other guys and never did anything except keep listening.... Doesn't seem likely."

"He might have cracked," Eunice said.

We nodded. People cracked. That happened on Lifetime all the time, too.

"Listen." Berks stood up. "We've got to do the right thing. Let's take the stuff down to the police station in the morning. My uncle's there. We'll talk to him. And we won't get in trouble because he does everything my mother tells him, and she won't want me to get in trouble."

"We do have that Halloween party to get to. I don't want to waste my costume," Eunice said.

Berks and I shrugged into our hippie clothes. A Halloween party with a bunch of other kids our age suddenly seemed pretty tame.

"I've got a better idea." I pulled on a sweatshirt. "Let's drive by Disco Donna's house."

I have no idea why it seemed like a good idea to go to Disco Donna's house or what we'd do when we got there, but five minutes later Eunice parked her mom's van in a pool of hazy gray light from the streetlight directly in front of the old Demonte house. Two large Dumpsters filled with rubble sat in a yard overgrown with weeds. Someone had left a lawn mower and a pile of equipment by the front door. There were only a few houses on this side of the park, and the laughter of trick-or-treaters on the main road was swallowed by the shadows lurking beyond the streetlight. We all had flashlights we'd found in the van, thanks to Eunice's mother, a Girl Scout leader.

"I am so not okay with this," Eunice said.

"Come on, I just want to take a look," I whispered as I drew closer to the house.

"Cluck, cluck." Berks laughed and pulled Eunice through a pile of dead leaves.

Vines twisted up a trellis to the Demontes' second floor. I aimed the flashlight at the trellis, spotlighting blackened petals and curved thorns. "The vines are roses! The killer probably got a rose from the trellis when he killed her!"

"I am waaay creeped out." Eunice shivered.

"Now that we're here, I want to see her room. Who's coming in?" In the light from my flashlight, Berks's eyes glowed.

"No freaking way." Eunice folded her arms.

"Don't worry, Eunice." I started walking around the house. "You can be the lookout. Down here. Alone. As in all by yourself. With the ghosts."

Eunice punched my shoulder but followed close behind as we crept into the backyard. We tried the door; it was locked, but being tall has its advantages. We pushed a trash can under a window. I climbed up on it and managed to slide a window open. I swung into the dark house and then opened the kitchen door for my friends. Inside, we bunched together and made our way down the hallway. Pale gray fingers of streetlight clawed at the dirty windows.

We OMG'd up the stairs.

Everything creaked. We peered into gutted rooms. The emptiness magnified our every gasping breath. As we passed a derelict bathroom, Eunice moaned, "I'll never get into Harvard with a rap sheet."

Berks hugged her. "No way my uncle will let this get out. Even if we get arrested, no worries, Eunice. Trust me."

I stopped at a door at the end of the hall. "I bet this was her room. It's on the side with the trellis."

"A psycho could climb up the rose trellis again. And kill an innocent high-school girl. What are we doing here again?" Eunice's voice wavered.

"We'll look fast." I turned the knob and the door creaked open.

"Two minutes," Eunice said. "I mean it."

Three beams of light crisscrossed silently in the empty room. I don't know what I expected—to see her room as it was? I had imagined a ruffled bed and painted furniture, kind of hippy colors, posters on the wall.

"Berks, what was that poster she had? The blond rock guy?"

"Frampton Comes Alive?" Berks whispered. Her fingers clamped so tight on my arm they were cutting off my circulation.

"Frampton Comes Alive? You mean Peter Frampton? My dad listens to that," Eunice said.

Berks's fingers tightened. "Maybe Peter…"

"Peter was the poster!" I said. "But how would a poster keep her secrets?"

"If this were my room, I'd put the bed here." Berks waved her hand like a spokesmodel on a game show. "There are all these eaves and windows, so the only wall for a bed is here." She turned. "And if I had a poster of a hot guy I wanted to see all the time, I'd put it…there." She waved to the wall with a built-in bookcase.

"It would have fit there," I said. We hurried to the empty bookcase and stared at the three-foot gap between the two middle shelves.

"Uh, what are we looking at?" Eunice's voice was getting shrill. "Bookshelves. Nothing to see here, people. Let's go!"

"Wait!" I started knocking on the back of the shelves. "On TV there's always a hiding place behind the wall."

Berks crouched down, aiming her light so I could see. The back of the bottom shelf made a different, hollow sound. "No way!" Berks said.

Eunice knelt too, her eyes wide, aiming her flashlight at the bottom shelf. Eunice pulled a Swiss Army knife from her key chain. "Finally something I can use this for." She knelt down and angled the knife into a seam at the back of the shelf. "It's coming away. It's just cardboard painted like the wood!"

The flashlight beams wavered as we jockeyed to see better. I pulled away crumbling cardboard. There was a narrow, hollowed-out space behind it. In it sat a small white cardboard gift box.

Berks reached into the bookcase. "Don't touch it," I whispered. "I'll get gloves—"

"What was that?" Eunice said in the loudest stage whisper I'd ever heard.

I'd heard it, too. A *thump* downstairs. Berks jumped to her feet.

"The lights," I said.

We switched off the flashlights. The thumping continued. I stood slowly. I could barely breathe. I could just see Berks's wide eyes in the pale light coming from the window. I could hear Eunice moaning. She reverted to Korean, which she did only when she was completely unhinged or in gym class. There was more thumping, and then a pungent smell, and then a *whoosh* and a reddish glow from the hall. Eunice and Berks jumped and shouted, "Fire!"

I ran to the door and saw a red glow and a cloud of white smoke surging toward us. I slammed the bedroom door shut and ran to the window. "If a psycho killer can climb the trellis in, we can climb out."

"You first!" Berks shrieked as I struggled to raise the sash.

The window groaned open. I swung one leg over the sill and aimed my flashlight beam onto the trellis. "Okay," I said. "Doable." Eunice and Berks held my arms while I hung from the sill, until my feet found the trellis. It creaked. I prayed it would hold me.

Smoke gathered behind Eunice and Berks.

I was carefully climbing down the trellis when I heard sirens shrieking. I twisted my head. A police car swung into the Demontes' driveway, followed by a fire engine. Firefighters leapt from the truck. A radio squawked, and one of the firefighters pointed to the side of the house. I hurried to the ground, then waved my flashlight and shouted. The firefighters reached the base of the trellis as Eunice neared the bottom. Berks quickly followed, touching the ground just as a police officer jogged up.

Berks shone her flashlight on her own face. "Hey, Uncle Paul, it's me, Berks."

Uncle Paul rubbed his face. His shoulders slumped. "I know," he muttered. He pulled us aside as firefighters placed ladders and started hoses. "Your mother tracked you on your cell phone. When she saw you weren't at the Halloween party, she called me."

Berks swore. "I am so dead."

A few minutes later we were hustled into the back of an ambulance, its back door left open, while the cops and Uncle Paul decided what to do with us. The firefighters quickly contained the fire. Nobody would tell us what was happening, but we caught words like "accelerant" and "dumbass prank."

"I guess I can kiss off Harvard." Eunice's eyes searched mine. "They can't pin this on us. Right?"

"Absolutely not," I said. "We didn't do it." I meant the fire. We had definitely broken into the house.

"Oh, my God." Berks pointed. "It just got worse. Look who just showed up. Principal Smith! He's over there talking with the cops."

We could see Principal Smith standing under the street lamp. He had smoke smudges on his shirt and bald head. A firefighter leaned into the ambulance and told us we were lucky. Principal Smith had been driving by and saw the fire. He'd gone into the house to make sure no one was trapped inside. Passing trick-or-treaters called the fire department.

Eunice moaned.

"We're doomed," Berks said. "And the worst part is, we'll never know what Disco Donna hid in the bookcase."

"Oh, yes we will." I pulled the cardboard box, now slightly crushed, from beneath my tie-dye T-shirt.

"Screw forensics," Eunice said. "Let's open that box."

Berks pulled the door to the ambulance shut. My hand shook as I lifted the lid of the box.

Inside was one dried rose, brownish gray and moldy. A cassette tape. And a shiny old Polaroid photograph. "Oh, my God," Berks exclaimed. "It's a naked guy! It's, it's…"

"Looks like he's asleep," Eunice whispered.

As I set down the lid of the box, I noticed something written on its underside.

The door jerked open. Uncle Paul looked in. "Well, what do you ladies have to say for yourselves?"

I turned the lid of the box so Berks and Eunice could see it.

Berks smiled. "Uncle Paul, you'd better get ready to make an arrest. We know who killed Disco Donna."

Uncle Paul didn't look too pleased, but he climbed in, closed the door, and listened. We told him what we had done, from the moment we found the hall pass. He kept rubbing his hand over his face, especially when we told him about entering the house, but then we showed him the box. With the rose. And the cassette. And the photo. And the lid of the box, where Donna had practiced her signature. Or what she thought would be her new signature.

Mrs. Cale Smith.

* * * *

Two nights later, Berks called to tell me the details of what Mrs. Maven had already reported at Cookie's. Brave Principal Smith, who had tried to rescue a bunch of honor-society arsonists, had been arrested.

The man in the photo, the man heard during a "romantic exchange" on the tape, was our principal. He'd been a gym teacher at Roseport High all those years ago. He'd left town shortly after Disco Donna's murder, but had returned to take a promotion to principal, thinking that no one would remember his brief time as a gym teacher at the same school nearly forty years before.

He'd been in Cookie's when Mrs. Maven made her broadcast about the hall pass. Creepiest of all, he confessed that he had followed us after seeing the "vision" of Donna in Retro Rags—my friend Berks, of course, wearing Donna's old dress. When he saw us going into the Demonte house and feared we might have found some evidence, he decided to burn the place—and us—down.

Needless to say, we all got grounded, except for our appearances on *Crime Solvers* and the *Today Show*.

We still tease Berks about the vision thing.

Eunice wouldn't speak to me for days, until Berks convinced her that our adventure would make a *killer* college-application essay.

Shari Randall still hasn't decided if she's a reader with a writing problem or a writer with a reading problem. She is a children's librarian and literacy advocate. If she is not traveling to some place warm, or haunting vintage clothing stores and antiques shops, she's probably dancing. She blogs at Writers Who Kill (www.writerswhokill.blogspot.com).

MONSTER PARTY

by Meg Opperman

During our annual Fourth of July barbeque, I steeled myself for the inevitable. It was getting so I dreaded the holidays, and that says something, because I am a holiday junkie. Any excuse to celebrate—Groundhog Day, Arbor Day, Memorial Day, Labor Day—you name it, I'll celebrate it.

As the day progressed, I surrounded myself with other party-goers, keeping a safe distance from Joseph Cozzaluccio's roaming hands. No doubt he'd manage to get a pinch or pat in at some point, anyway. Coach Joe is an octopus in a track suit. He's also the closest thing my husband, Rick, has to a father.

"He's harmless," Rick has said many times. Or, "Jeanie, he just lost Nina. Can't you show a little compassion?" So he continues to bring Coach Joe over every—and I mean *every*—holiday. Joe arrives with a six-pack of beer, lots of hugs and kisses for the kids, and a big appetite.

At Christmas it was "Jeanie, we're under the mistletoe," as he held a wilted sprig over my head. On Valentine's Day, it was a pat on the bottom and a "Who needs a box of chocolates?" Saint Patrick's Day brought a pinch on the cheek and "Oops. My eyesight must be shot, I didn't see you were wearing green." At Easter, the accidental brush-up as we passed in the hallway. Accidentally, *five times*. And after every grope he'd wink and add, "I just miss you so, Jeanie."

I don't like to complain, but he was ruining my perfect holidays, dead wife or not. I'd finally begged Rick to talk to Coach Joe about keeping his tentacles to himself. I wasn't sure Rick would do it, but if he didn't, I'd have to handle Coach Joe myself.

As the Fourth wore on, I became more and more tense. I snapped at Rick by the punch bowl, and I raised my voice to Spencer when he and his friends got too rowdy. I chastised Haley for her too-revealing tube top. When had she become so…developed? Kyle, the Milners' boy, practically had his tongue lolling out. At one point, my brother even asked if something was wrong, since I'd tuned out while he told a particularly witty story, and an old sorority sister asked if my monthly friend was visiting.

When Rick and Coach Joe headed into the shed to work on their latest fix-it project—a bookshelf that Rick made when we first married—I relaxed, I smiled, I laughed.

Later, at the kitchen sink, I felt strong arms go around my waist. I tensed, ready to give Coach Joe an earful.

"Tough day?" Rick whispered, his breath stirring the hairs on my neck.

Leaning into him, I gave his arm a squeeze. "Thought you and Coach Joe were fixing a bookshelf."

"Just checking in to see if you need me to do anything," he said, kissing my earlobe, his arms tightening on my waist. "I talked to Joe. You shouldn't have any more…problems."

"Wonderful! You're amazing!" I exhaled, tension easing from my muscles.

"How amazing?" Rick's lips moved to my neck.

"We have guests," I said, a little breathless. "And what about Joe? He's waiting for you."

"The kids are keeping him company.…Thought we could start the fireworks early."

As if summoned, Spencer burst into the kitchen, followed by several friends. "Ewww!" they shouted in unison as they caught us kissing.

"Out!" Rick hollered, but he grinned as he said it.

"Go back to your shed, sweetheart." I laughed.

A perfect day.

* * * *

When the party wound down, Rick drove Coach Joe home. Not a pinch, a poke, or a pat. Not even a "I just miss you so, Jeanie." And a good-as-new bookcase. Best holiday ever! I hummed as I collected empty bottles, threw away cups and plates, and wrapped up leftovers.

Across the street, Kyle slouched on his front porch, easily recognizable in the growing dark. Last year he'd been a short, sweet, pudgy kid with a huge crush on Haley. This summer it looked like he'd fallen into a taffy-stretching machine. Somewhere along the way, he'd also forgotten the address of his barber and had started wearing those low-slung jeans that are supposed to be cool—I called them indecent—with the kids. He still had a crush on Haley, though. And lately she had seemed to return his interest.

"Did you enjoy the party, Kyle?" I called out.

He shrugged, then trudged into his house, closing the door with a *thump*.

Perhaps his manners had been stretched right out of him, too?

When Rick returned, I urged the kids to hurry so we could get to the special spot where we always watched Baltimore's fireworks display. I loved the spectacle. We all did. Spencer bounded down the stairs, but surprisingly, no Haley.

"Haley!" I shouted up to her again.

"Staying home," she called back.

"Come on, Haley-Bear," Rick said. "The fireworks are going to be amazing this year."

When Haley didn't answer, I started up the steps. Was she sick? Had she snuck into the adults-only punch?

Rick laid a hand on my wrist, shook his head. "Welcome to the moods of a mercurial thirteen-year-old, Jeanie. Let her be."

I paused on the stairs for a moment, unsure. We'd never left her by herself for long and I knew we'd be gone for more than an hour. "Maybe I should stay home, too."

"She's okay, hon. Let her grow up a little. We'll be back before she even has time to miss us."

* * * *

The day after the Fourth, Haley padded downstairs around lunchtime wearing one of her dad's T-shirts and an oversized pair of sweats. She slumped in a kitchen chair—at this rate she'd be hunchbacked by sixteen—and didn't say a word. I put a grilled cheese sandwich and a mug of homemade tomato soup on the counter in front of her.

"You okay, honey?" I straightened my shoulders. Would she get the hint?

A grunt, her only answer. Her fingers dissected the sandwich, pulling the cheese from the center, like she used to do when she was little. Her soup untouched.

"What's wrong, sweetie? You have a fight with Kyle?" When she didn't reply, I said, "Maybe sitting up straight would make you feel better."

Haley glanced up from her sandwich long enough to give me an impressive eye roll.

Having a teenage daughter is enough to make you want to pull your hair out strand by strand. Haley had always been a bubbly kid, but since she'd hit thirteen, she'd become downright sullen. She'd have frown lines if she didn't watch out, and Botox was expensive.

“Haley-Bear,” Rick said as he came into the kitchen carrying the newspaper, “I’m not going to have anything to wear if you keep raiding my closet.”

She colored. “Well, Mom won’t buy me new clothes, and I don’t like my old ones anymore.”

This was news to me. “What do you mean you don’t like them?”

Sighing as though she were talking to a half-wit, she said, “They’re too…girly.”

Rick looked up from his paper. “And here I thought they were just too tight.”

“*Daaad*!” She burst into tears and ran upstairs. We heard her bedroom door slam.

“What on earth—”

“Jeanie, wait. Let me go talk to her.” Rick put down the paper and sighed. “Remember when she could take a joke?”

I shrugged. What could I say?

* * * *

That August, we went back-to-school shopping, and all Haley’s clothing choices were varying shades of black. Still tight, but nothing remotely girly. Later that month, she and her best friend, Maya, went full-blown Goth. They spent their allowance on hair color, and Haley dyed her beautiful, long brown hair flat black. They then chopped it at sharp, uneven angles. I thought Rick would have a coronary when he saw what she’d done to herself. They didn’t speak for a week.

Then in September, Haley wanted to skip our Labor Day festivities—parade, carnival, and afterward barbequing with our neighbors and, of course, Coach Joe. I loved Labor Day. We all did.

Instead, she asked to go to Maya’s house for the day.

Rick frowned. In a sharp voice that he rarely used—especially with our daughter—he said, “You know, Haley Elizabeth, sometimes you have to spend time with family. That’s how it goes. Maya’s house will be there tomorrow or the next day.”

“But *Daaad*,” she whined. When she saw he wasn’t going to budge, she turned to me. “*Please*, Mom. I’ll spend all day with you guys tomorrow, I promise. Maya has tickets to—”

“No, your dad’s right, Haley. Family time.”

“It’s not fair!” She spun around and ran back up the stairs. We winced when the door slammed.

* * * *

Spencer jumped up and down, waving to all the passing floats at the parade. It wasn't so long ago that Haley would have joined him. Instead, she sat on a curb and texted with friends. When her dad got fed up and pocketed the phone, she screamed, "I hate you!" and turned her back on us.

At the carnival, she barely spoke, except when Kyle marched over, his shoulders stooped, stringy bangs all but hiding his eyes.

"We need to talk," he said, as if the rest of us weren't there.

"Go away, I'm not speaking to you," she snapped.

"But—"

"Sooo outta here." She stormed off down the sidewalk.

I noticed Kyle's lower lip tremble. What had he done to make her so angry?

"I'm sorry," Rick said, "I don't know what's gotten into her."

I pressed my lips together tightly. *Her*? What about Kyle? Surely this was *his* fault!

"Whatever." Kyle slouched off in the opposite direction.

I made a mental note to call his mother about his lack of manners. I was sure she'd want to know.

Later, Rick tried to cheer Haley up by challenging her to a carnival game of her choosing. She shook her head.

"That's baby stuff, Dad."

Baby stuff? Since when was spending time with family "baby stuff"?

By the time we got home to prepare for the barbeque, we were both about to wring Haley's neck.

"Mom?" Haley entered the kitchen where the brats were simmering in beer and I was stirring the potato salad.

"Hmm?" A little more salt for the salad, and it would be blue-ribbon perfect. Just the way I liked it.

"I don't feel good. I'm going to lie down for a while." Her voice scratchy, hands on her belly.

"What's wrong, honey? Is this about Kyle? You don't *have* to spend time with him at the party—"

"I just don't like him anymore, okay? Will you drop it?" Her voice cracked. "A stomachache, that's all. Must be the carnival food or something."

* * * *

Our neighbors arrived, which included the Milners, who practically had to drag Kyle along, his face set in sullen lines. Somehow he'd become a kid I didn't know and wasn't sure I liked.

Soon after, Rick returned with Coach Joe and his six-pack. They were already talking sports, Spencer in tow.

"Where's Haley?" Coach Joe asked, neglecting to greet me.

"Not feeling well," Rick replied. "Stomachache."

"That's too bad. Maybe I should go say hello, see how she's doing?" He inched toward the stairs.

I called out, "Don't waste your time, Joe. She doesn't like anyone in her room these days."

Rick rolled his eyes. "You can say that again. She doesn't seem to like anyone, period."

Coach Joe shrugged. "Teenagers. What can you do? Remember the time…" and he and Rick went off on another trip down memory lane as they headed to the shed to set up their latest repair project—an old rocking chair that I'd used to lull the kids to sleep when they were babies.

* * * *

A little later, I watched Kyle slip into our house with some of the other boys. When he didn't come back out with his pals when the burgers came off the grill, I excused myself from the party. I stopped to grab a heating pad and a bottle of Midol from the bathroom, and went to check on Haley. Had Kyle gone home or up to Haley's room to try to mend fences? Or…maybe for something else?

As I hurried to the top of the steps and turned into the hall, I saw Coach Joe—not Kyle—standing in front of Haley's door, holding a can of soda and jiggling the door knob.

"Come on, honey, let ol' Coach Joe in," he crooned. "I brought you a Coke."

"Leave me alone, *please*," Haley pleaded in a timid voice I hardly recognized as my daughter's.

"I just miss you so, Haley," he said.

"What are you…" I gasped.

Coach Joe turned and pasted on a harmless grin. "Hey, Jeanie. Just checking on Haley. Still not feeling well, I think."

He shuffled past but didn't touch me. He didn't notice my knuckles whitening as I gripped the heating pad in a stranglehold.

* * * *

A few days before Halloween, our power went out in a Frankenstorm. Rain pelted our neighborhood for a day and a half, and high winds toppled a few of our older trees, one even grazing our roof. Most of Maryland weathered the storm well, but being so near the coast, our neighborhood wasn't so lucky.

We still didn't have power on Halloween, but fortunately Rick had installed a sizable generator inside the shed after we'd survived Snowmageddon two years before. That evening, we switched it over to run the outside lights. I wasn't crazy about the noise it made, but I'd had plenty of time to get used to it over the previous couple of days. Besides, several other neighbors ran theirs, too. So we were in good company.

Usually, we would go trick-or-treating together—a chance to show off our costumes—while Coach Joe stayed back and handed out candy to the neighborhood kids. I'd spent weeks designing and sewing costumes for our theme—monster party—and they were some of the best I'd ever made. I dressed as the bride of Frankenstein in a low-cut, satiny gown. Rick got the honor of being the monster himself, while Spencer was wrapped head-to-toe as a mummy. I'd made a girl-zombie costume for Haley. I'd even sewn an extra-bloody vampire suit for Coach Joe.

Haley loved Halloween. We all did. But this year she'd shown zero interest in pumpkin-carving, trick-or-treating, or helping me put together the costumes.

Earlier in the day, Haley had come into the living room, looking glum. "Mom, Dad, please, I don't want to go trick-or-treating. Can't I go to Maya's?"

I started to nod, but Rick barked, "No way, Haley. You may not like it, but you *are* part of this family. You're going—"

"Actually, I think we should let her go, hon."

Both of them turned to stare at me openmouthed.

"What did you say?" Rick asked.

"I talked to Maya's mother last night, and it seems they've entered a costume contest at her work. They're going as the Zombie Family Robinson—I know, a clever play on their last name—and they could use one more zombie."

"And you'd be willing to let Haley go?" His eyes narrowed. Boy, did he know me well.

"At first I wasn't open to it, but when I found out first prize is a gift certificate and an appointment for four at that new day spa I've been trying to get into, and Maya's mom is willing to share..."

"You're giving our daughter up for a hair appointment?"

"Antoine's supposed to be amazing," I gushed. "And it's just this one time. They're sure to win. Did you see the amount of work I put into that costume?"

* * * *

I dropped Haley off long before Rick went to pick up Coach Joe. As we pulled into Maya's driveway, Haley turned to me.

"Thanks for letting me go, Mom. I know you like us all together for holidays."

"It's just this one time, okay?" I adjusted her collar to make sure the bloody gash I'd painted would show.

She leaned over and kissed me on the cheek, something she hadn't done in months.

"Aw, don't go ruining your makeup." I smiled. "Have a good time."

After returning home, I put on my own costume and twirled in front of a full-length mirror. Nice.

When I shimmied out to the shed an hour later, Coach Joe all but ignored me, even with my impressive cleavage. He and Rick were completing this year's lawn decoration, a motion-activated Frankenstein monster, rising from its coffin. Every year we added a piece to our graveyard scene.

The men took their time positioning the decorations and spotlights just so on the lawn. When they finished and went off to share a beer, I checked their work and made a small adjustment, just to ensure everything was perfect.

After wrapping Spencer into his costume, we managed to get out of the house, leaving Coach Joe at home to distribute the candy. Hundreds of candles lit up our neighborhood and—for those of us with generators—lights. No one wanted to miss trick-or-treating and the chance to show off their displays. My kind of place.

As we headed down the driveway, I rubbed my eyes. Then rubbed them some more. Tears began to roll down my cheeks. "Rick," I said, "I think I'm having a reaction to the makeup."

My husband turned and flashed his light in my face. "Jesus, Jeanie, your eyes are bright red. You better wash that stuff off quick." He moved to help me back to the house, but I waved him off.

"You go on with Spencer. I'll wash up and help Coach Joe with the candy."

"Come on, Dad!" Spencer tugged on his arm. I waved and stuffed my hand in my costume's pocket, checking the jalapeño pepper slice concealed there.

Hurrying up the drive and into the house, I breezed past Coach Joe, heading for the kitchen sink where I rinsed my eyes and washed away all traces of my carefully applied makeup. A small sacrifice. Once that was done, I returned to the front door and waited while Coach Joe gave fistfuls of candy to some passing kids.

When the kids disappeared down the sidewalk, I explained about the bad reaction to my makeup and that I'd be staying to help.

I scanned the yard, pointed to the new decoration. "Oh no, look at the coffin lid! It isn't moving. Those kids must have broken it. Rick will be so upset."

Coach Joe followed my finger to the Frankenmonster. He squinted. "Where?"

We went into the yard to check out the damage.

"I can fix this, easy," Coach Joe said. "Just help me carry it to the shed."

"Really? You'd do that?"

"Of course!"

Together we managed to wrestle the coffin into the shed.

Turning the light on, I said, "I'll go back and hand out candy. Let me know when you're done."

He waved absently, already involved in his project.

Exiting, I shut the door, then quietly snapped on the padlock. I stood there a moment, taking cleansing breaths. Earlier, I'd put a couple of all-but-invisible slits in the generator's carbon monoxide exhaust hose. Would Coach Joe notice?

Fixing a smile on my face, I returned to the house to hand out candy for another hour. When there was a lull in trick-or-treaters, I slipped back out, returned to the shed. A thin trail of exhaust spiraled from under the door as the generator droned on. Almost too easy. I removed the padlock. This was one vampire who would never again suck the life from someone. Too bad about the lawn ornament, though. But Rick could fix it for next year.

"Oh, I'll just miss you so, Joe," I said under my breath.

With new buoyancy in my step, I returned to the house, then handled the trick-or-treaters until Rick and Spencer returned. It wasn't long before Rick asked where Coach Joe had gotten to, and I explained about the kids breaking our lawn decoration. He ambled out to the shed.

A few minutes later, he came running in, his face white even under the monster makeup, tears in his eyes.

"Call 9-1-1!" he cried. "The generator—"

* * * *

On Thanksgiving, my brother and his family came to dinner. After I pulled the turkey out of the oven, I called upstairs to the kids. Spencer and the cousins rushed down as if they hadn't eaten in months. I waited for Haley to make an appearance, too. After a couple of minutes, I called up again. Kyle was on his way to spend Thanksgiving at his grandmother's, but had stopped by to see her before they left town. Haley had miraculously started speaking to him again, and—while she didn't ever say anything about it—I figured with Coach Joe gone a great weight had been lifted and she was more open to boys' attentions.

Kyle fidgeted as he stood by me at the bottom of the stairs, continually swiping hair out of his eyes. After the third time calling her, Haley bounded down the steps wearing skinny jeans and a bright pink T-shirt that hovered just north of her belly button. Her hair, now cut into a glossy brown bob—Antoine was worth every penny—looked very feminine.

"Wow." Kyle straightened to his full height.

He was almost handsome when he didn't stoop...but not as clean-cut and attractive as the Pattersons' boy, an all-state junior at Haley's school, who I'd heard had recently asked her out.

"Wow, yourself," Haley said, a big smile on her face.

If it saddened Rick to notice Coach Joe's absence at the table, Haley's grin was the best salve. He cleared his throat. "I think you forgot to put on a shirt, Haley-Bear."

She laughed and ran back upstairs to change.

Did I mention that we all love Thanksgiving? I took Rick's hand, gave it a squeeze. Everything was nearly perfect. My eyes strayed to Kyle.

But there's always room for improvement.

Meg Opperman penned her first mystery in the sixth grade. The protagonist was a dog named Smokey. Having moved on from her four-footed friend, she has written several short stories that actually have people in them. (Believe me, it's better this way.) A cultural anthropologist by training, Meg has mastered the art of eavesdropping in bars around the globe and being an unabashed snoop who's always in search of a story. She's currently at work on an urban fantasy novel set in D.C.

SHADOW BOXER

by Carla Coupe

I paused on the opposite curb and smoothed my long, black gloves. The place looked the same, all clapboards and gingerbread, two big plate-glass windows cleverly added to show off the current crop of offerings. Peter had hung a new sign above the door, acid green and black: Gallerie D'Orsay. I would've chosen a different typeface—that Art Nouveau font was overused and commercial.

The crowd entering was the usual mix of young and old, wealthy and student-poor. Some wore Halloween costumes, others dressed for an evening of gallery-hopping. Even from a distance, they reeked of pretension.

Stop it. That's not what I'm here for.

I took a steadying breath and adjusted my black, satin mask. It covered most of my face, leaving just my eyes and scarlet-painted mouth visible. As I crossed the street, I dodged cars and SUVs that inched along, scouting for parking spots. The crowd swept me through the heavy doors and into the gallery.

Young women dressed in tattered bustiers and bustles—zombie can-can dancers?—handed out black plastic glasses of white wine and, in fake French accents, directed newcomers to tables spread with finger-foods.

My hands shook when I took a glass, so I set it down on a tray filled with empties. *Don't lose your edge now.*

At the entrance to the room on the left, Peter had placed a placard on a stand, his usual grudging concession to publicity:

Exhibit Opening Halloween

Windows to the Macabre

Assemblages by Jonas Brewster

My heart battered against my breastbone. I lifted my chin and walked into the room.

Shadowboxes—foot square, wooden boxes painted black, open on one side like the shoebox dioramas we used to make in grade school—covered the walls and sat grouped on display pedestals. Each was carefully lit from inside. Peepholes to a strange world.

I turned to the shadowbox on my right, labeled with a small "first." Of course. Calling it "one" would be too lowbrow for Jonas. Inside, a child sat up in bed, staring at a luminous shape in the corner of its bedroom—a guardian angel being devoured by a demon. The figures and furnishings were crafted from bits of costume jewelry, old buttons and clasps, disassembled watches and cell phones. The detritus of modern life.

The babble of voices faded. Moving from shadowbox to shadowbox, following the story of the demon-haunted child, I finally reached the last one, labeled forty-ninth. No need to look; I knew how the tale ended. Beneath my mask, sweat trickled down my cheeks and salt stung my eyes.

Bright light suddenly flooded a corner of the room. I edged through the crush. A tall, black-clad guy pointed a news camera at a woman in a pomegranate-red suit holding a microphone.

Who had Peter bribed to get television news coverage? But no, he'd never pay for it; he'd think it was his by right. Probably part of the town's Gallery Walk publicity.

The reporter's mouth moved as she gestured toward the display, her words lost in the hubbub.

Then *he* stepped into the light.

Jonas.

The crowd stilled as the reporter spoke again, and Jonas smiled. *That* smile. The bashful, gee-whiz, look-at-me-I'm-so-modest one. He added an artful shrug and lifted his eyebrows for good measure before growing serious and indicating a shadowbox on the wall labeled "twenty-third."

The one where the child, now grown, tries to commit suicide for the first time.

Jonas spoke for a minute or two, all brooding intensity in his dark silk shirt and neatly pressed designer jeans.

"Thank you, Jonas Brewster," the reporter said. "I urge everyone to come and see this extraordinary exhibit before it moves on. This is Sally Hobbes saying happy Halloween."

When she nodded, the camera light went out.

The crowd shifted, broke around me like water around a pebble in a stream. Now that the excitement of filming was over, people moved back toward the wine and hors d'oeuvre tables in the entry.

I gazed at the familiar figure in shadowbox twenty-third and twisted a lock of blond hair around my fingers.

"Laura?" Jonas stood beside me, jaw tight, nostrils flaring. "Thought it was you. I'd recognize that cloak and elf-wannabe get-up anywhere. What the hell are you doing here?" He bit off the words, one by one, but kept his voice soft. "You're not my girlfriend anymore. I told you what would happen if you came back."

I swallowed, my throat like sandpaper.

A smile stretched his lips, as fake as his teeth, and he reached for me. "If you think I'm going to let you ruin my big chance…"

With a gasp, I turned and fled.

People clogged the door—witches, vampires, fairies, a man in an Andy Warhol wig—but I slipped through them and gained the sidewalk. I shivered in the cool air, a welcome contrast to the stifling heat of the gallery, and hurried down the block, glancing over my shoulder. Jonas emerged from the gallery, hesitated on the threshold, scanning the street, then sauntered down the steps toward me.

Joining a cluster of gallery-goers, I tried to blend in. No way did I believe Jonas was just out for a stroll. He was following me. I had to stay around people, not let him get me alone.

The squat brick building housing Roberts Fine Art appeared on my right. The crowds weren't as thick here—too avant-garde to appeal to most—but decent wine and plentiful hors d'oeuvres attracted those in the know. I slipped inside.

Waving away the offer of another wine-filled plastic glass, I paused before a huge canvas, but my attention stayed fixed on the door.

Sure enough, Jonas entered, ignoring the young man who greeted him, heading straight for me.

I ducked into the next room and threaded through people standing around trays heaped with cheese and vegetables. The rooms all interconnected, allowing a circular flow, and I reached the outer door as Jonas rounded a corner.

Then I was back on the crowded sidewalk.

The next gallery, Betty's Baubles, housed one big room filled with display cases of jewelry. I moved from case to case, heading toward the rear, while Jonas lounged on the front stoop, checking his phone, waiting. He caught my gaze through the glass door and the corners of his mouth curled up, but there was nothing friendly in his expression.

My hands shook.

Three quick steps and I entered the short hall to the bathroom and kitchenette. A cinder block propped open the back door.

The front door chimed. Footsteps thudded on the hardwood floor.

"Hey, Jonas, congratulations! We didn't expect to see you—"

"Yeah, thanks, man. Catch you later," he said.

I had already reached the edge of the employee parking lot when he hurried out the door, head turning. When he caught sight of me, he deliberately rubbed his crotch, and my skin crawled.

A quick right turn and I took off down a dark, narrow passage between buildings. About halfway, I glanced over my shoulder and pulled up short.

Jonas had disappeared. Had he dashed around the building to ambush me as I reached the street? Was he back in the parking lot, waiting for me to retrace my steps? Or had he given up the chase?

I pressed against the wall, my harsh gasps loud in my ears. What should I do?

He'd find it easier to hide with all those cars in the parking lot, so I'd have a better chance of spotting him if I continued on to the road. At least there wasn't a street or shop light right at the end of the passage.

I pulled the hood of my cloak over my head and tucked away a few stray blond strands. Right now, shadows were my friends. Then I crept forward, listening for footsteps, craning my neck, trying to keep an eye in front as well as behind.

At the mouth of the passage, I paused. Groups of people passed by. If I could join one…

I edged out of the darkness.

Fingers closed around my arm. My heart stuttered; a scream died in my throat.

"I thought you were smarter than this, Laura," Jonas whispered, his breath hot against my face, his fingers tightening, pale against the black of my cloak. "Guess I need to teach you another lesson."

"No, don't," I breathed, barely audible, as I trembled and blinked away tears. He slung one arm over my shoulders, pressing me close, and pulled me down the street, dodging the crowds. An unlit black bulk loomed on our left.

"Look, there's St. Catherine's," he said. He brushed his lips against my neck. I wanted to peel off my skin. "They're doing construction on the church building, but the graveyard's the same. Remember when I fucked you against a headstone? Think I'll do it again. It'll be just like old times."

"Please…"

Under my cloak, his hand roamed over my breast, and I squirmed in his grasp. When we were across the street from the church, I took a deep breath, reached up and unfastened the cloak's clasp at my throat, and jerked away. His arm slipped off my shoulders. He grabbed at me, fingers clutching my clothes, but I pulled free. I darted through the traffic to the opposite sidewalk with Jonas close behind.

A honk, two. "Fuck off," Jonas shouted at a driver who just missed him. He banged his hand on the car's trunk.

I dashed toward the unlit church and, ignoring the "Keep Out" sign, dodged through a gap in the chain-link fence. Behind me, the squeal of brakes and a string of curses tracked his progress.

My footsteps crunched on the gravel path as I headed along the side of the church to the back. A quick turn, gravel spraying, and I ran up a set of stairs that ended on a wide stone porch about ten feet off the ground, overlooking the graveyard. The church's heavy wooden door broke the expanse of worn brick on my right. Iron railings bordering the porch had been removed, replaced by ubiquitous orange construction webbing. Dim light filtered through the branches of the trees that surrounded the building, striping the stone with a moving mosaic. At the far end of the porch, I turned and leaned against the brick wall, trying to catch my breath.

He skidded to a stop at the top of the stairs.

"Stupid as always, Laura," he said. "Running into a dead end. Almost as if you *want* me to catch you." He paused. "Yeah. That's it. You *do* want me to catch you."

I shook my head.

"Now you're lying." He laughed, hands on hips. "Admit it. You like it rough. You've *always* liked it rough. A little pain—a *lot* of pain—turns you on. Makes you more creative."

He swaggered as he approached. I shrank back.

"Those shadowboxes are your best work," he said. "*My* best work, really, since I'm the one who…motivated you."

A whimper escaped my throat.

"But now I've got my break," he continued. "TV coverage, a magazine article, even the Museum of Modern Art's interested in showing the boxes. I don't need you anymore." He lifted a fist. "So stay away if you know what's good for you. Keep your mouth shut. They're mine now."

"No," I whispered.

"Yes. Even if you told the whole world you created them, no one would believe you." He chuckled and ran his fingers through his hair, then shoved his hands in his pockets, a familiar gesture. "Who would *you* believe? Some crazy chick hanger-on, a *groupie*, or a guy with a proven track record? A guy with a dozen gallery shows to his credit?"

He stopped in front of me, hips cocked, hands still in his pockets. A shaft of light moved over his face, caught his grin.

Sliding over the rough brick, my fingers found and then tightened around the ring of heavy plastic hooked on the wall beside me. I grabbed the ring, the loop dropped over his head, and I pulled tight. He lunged forward, stopped short by the rope that was attached to the ring. The rope whose other end was tied to a high branch in the tree behind Jonas.

He gasped, fingers clawing at his neck.

"Don't bother." I stood tall, arms crossed over my chest. "It works like a zip tie. You can't loosen it. You have to cut it off."

He snarled, grabbed my hair.

I jumped back. He stared at the mask and blond wig hanging limply from his fingers.

Then he looked at me, eyes wide.

"Karen?"

"Congratulations. You finally figured it out," I said. "You're so predictable, Jonas. Laura told me what you did to her here, how you liked to return to the same spot. That made it easy for me to lead you into my trap…and to let you think you were leading me."

"What…" He dropped the mask and wig, tried to force a finger between the plastic loop and his neck.

I pulled a scrap of paper from my pocket, held it up. "Laura's obituary. It only appeared in our local paper, so you won't have seen it. My sister killed herself last week. Because of you."

Before he could reply, I stepped forward and crammed the obit into his shirt pocket.

"A pity you can't live without her, isn't it?"

I shoved him hard. He stumbled, took a step backward into nothing, and fell off the porch.

The rope tightened. A branch creaked. And Jonas swung beneath the trees, hands flailing, choked gasps almost drowned out by the rustle of dry leaves.

His struggles grew sluggish, more uncoordinated. After what seemed like ages, finally, *finally*, his arms flopped to his sides, his legs stopped twitching, and his light-dappled body swung in a gentle arc. A pendulum, slowly tallying the moments since his death.

I scooped up the wig and mask. Glancing back at the body, *his* body, I remembered the image in the final shadowbox: the demon-haunted child, now an adult, hanging from a tree branch.

Just as my little sister had done.

Just as Jonas did now.

Carla Coupe fell into writing short stories almost without noticing. Two of her short stories—"Rear View Murder" in *Chesapeake Crimes II* and "Dangerous Crossing" in *Chesapeake Crimes 3*—were nominated for Agatha Awards. Her Sherlock Holmes pastiches appear in *Sherlock Holmes Mystery Magazine* and *Sherlock's Home: The Empty House*.

LAST RITES

by Timothy Bentler-Jungr

Our part of Chelsea is not particularly kid friendly, so the doorbell caught me by surprise. Jason and Emmet had come by with little Maya a few hours before—her pink princess ensemble included a feather boa left over from Jason's *La Cage* phase—and I figured that was probably it for trick-or-treaters this year.

A few blocks away the clubs would be jammed with writhing bodies, of course. Not my scene anymore. Not since Eric had come into my life and showed me that domestic bliss wasn't simply a lie made up by Martha Stewart to sell magazines. I'd just poured myself a second glass of pinot noir and resumed surfing through the night's assortment of look-alike reality shows, wishing Eric was home to provide his scathing running commentary. I hit the mute button, grabbed a couple organic granola bars from the kitchen, and opened the door.

"Hello, Stephen."

Maybe it was the shock, or maybe it was how old and shrunken she looked, but it took a few beats for my brain to register what I was seeing. Not a little bed-sheet ghost, or a miniature Darth Vader. A real monster. The Wicked Witch of Long Island.

"Mom? What are you…I mean, how did…" I realized I was stammering like an idiot. I took a deep breath and pulled myself together. "How did you get here?"

It seemed like the simplest question to go with.

"Taxi." She must have caught me glancing up and down the block. "I sent him away already. So you'd have to invite me in."

An icy wind shrieked between the brownstones, scattering dead leaves and bits of rubbish in its wake. "I could leave you out on the stoop to freeze."

She seemed to consider this possibility for a moment. "That would be one way, I suppose. But I don't think you will. You aren't cruel."

And how would you know? I wanted to ask her. *I could be Jack-the-Friggin'-Ripper for all you know*. Call *me* cruel? She had kicked me out at sixteen and told me never to darken her door again. Her actual words. “Never darken my door again.” Geraldine O’Connor had always had a flair for the dramatic, if a little clichéd.

In twenty-two years, I hadn’t been anywhere near her door; now here she was, darkening mine. In all that time, I’d seen her once. Seven—no, eight—years ago, at Dad’s funeral. Even then, elegantly bereaved in black Chanel across a crowded church, she hadn’t spoken to me, hadn’t acknowledged my presence at all. Why now?

“I’ll call you another cab. But only because Lisa would kill me if anything happened to you.” I couldn’t make myself actually invite her in, but I stepped back and let her step into the foyer. “Don’t take your coat off. You won’t be staying that long.”

In the light of the hallway I got a better look at her. Her once beautiful face looked pale and hollowed out, with purplish circles around her eyes and sores on her lips. Her hands shook as she adjusted her wig. *Cranial prosthesis*, I corrected myself. According to my sister, that’s what you called it if you wanted insurance to cover it.

“May I sit down? All those steps, I’m a little winded.”

Before I could answer, she walked into the living room and sat down. First rule with door-to-door salesmen, don’t let them get their foot in the door. I’d blown it.

But that didn’t mean I’d buy whatever she was selling.

Eric’s antique armchair seemed to swallow her up, making her look like a child dressed up in her grandmother’s clothes. Trick or treat.

“Very nice,” she said, her pale-blue eyes taking in the room. “Classy. Not quite what I expected.”

“And what were you expecting?”

“I don’t know. Leather and rainbows, I suppose. This is so normal.”

“Sorry to disappoint you.”

“No, no, it’s nice. Cozy. Much more comfortable than Lisa’s place, with the toys everywhere. Is *he* here?” she asked, her voice dropping. “What do you call him? Your partner? Lover?”

“Eric. His name is Eric. And no, he’s not here. He’s in Boston all week, for work.”

“Oh, too bad.” She sounded genuinely disappointed. “I would have liked to meet him. Lisa says he’s very nice.”

“We’ve been together more than four years. Almost five. You’ve had plenty of time to meet him if you wanted to.” I realized I still had the granola bars in my clenched hand, crushed to crumbs inside their wrappers.

“True.” She heaved an operatic sigh. “But not much time left.”

More drama. “Spare me the pity party.”

“I don’t want your pity.”

"Then what do you want?"

"A glass of water, if you don't mind. It'll be time for my meds soon."

That threw me off guard. I spent a lot more time than necessary in the kitchen, fixing her a Perrier with ice and a twist of lemon while I tried to get my head around the situation. What the hell was she doing here?

"Thank you." Her hands quivered as she raised the glass to her lips, spilling a few drops on the front of her coat. "Do you have a coaster? I wouldn't want to ruin this lovely table."

"It was Eric's grandmother's," I told her as I placed the coaster in front of her.

"Ah. I'm to infer from that that his family didn't disown him?"

"His parents were here for Sunday dinner last week."

"That's…that's nice. Oh, for God's sake, Stephen, sit down. Let me look at you."

I sat on the sofa, facing her across the coffee table. My knee-jerk obedience annoyed me.

"You look good."

No thanks to you. "You look awful."

I don't know what surprised me more. That she laughed, or that it sounded just like it always had. I would've expected a cackle, I suppose, since she looked like she'd crawled out of the bad end of one of Grimm's grimmer fairy tales. "Oh, Stephen. You could always make me laugh."

For half a heartbeat I flashed back to when I was about seven or eight, the two of us cracking up over some silly joke. But the next heartbeat brought other flashbacks. "Not always."

"You're right." She sobered. "It's too late for pretence. For being nice. I appreciate your honesty."

"Good. Then maybe you can cut the crap. Why are you here?"

She drew a small pharmacy bottle out of her purse and handed it to me. "Could you open this for me? Damn child-proof caps."

Her helplessness disarmed me a little. Showing weakness had never been her style.

"How many?" I asked, twisting the cap.

"Two. No, better make it three, just to be safe."

I set three large, oval tablets on the table next to her glass. "You didn't come all the way over here so I could open your pills. What do you want?"

She took her time answering, swallowing the tablets one by one. "Is it so hard to believe I wanted to see my son?"

"A little bit, yeah. Why?"

"Don't be obtuse, Stephen. You know that I've been…that I'm ill. I know Lisa has kept you informed."

"If you're after bone marrow or a kidney or something, you've come to the wrong place."

"Nothing so dramatic as that." The last pill seemed to go down hard. She grimaced. "I've had a lot of time to think recently. To reflect on my life. *Examination of conscience*, that's what the nuns called it."

"Before confession. I remember." I hadn't been to church in ages, but some things were so drilled in you never forgot them. "Does that mean you're here for absolution? Fat chance. There's a church two blocks from here. Take a left at the corner. Try your luck there."

"Just hear me out, that's all I ask."

"What makes you think I want to hear anything you have to say?"

"Well, for one thing, you haven't called that cab yet."

I stood and crossed the room, heading toward the phone. "I'll get on that right now. The sooner you're out of here, the better."

"Wait, Stephen!" Something in her voice made me stop and look back. She had risen from the chair, but was now hunched over, her face white and rigid with pain.

I froze, unable to look away. Lisa had described Mom's illness in lurid detail. It was a way of unburdening herself from the stress of care-giving, I guess. But seeing it, seeing the agony Mom was in, I wasn't prepared for that.

"Shouldn't you be in a hospital or something?" Maybe I needed to call an ambulance instead of a cab.

"No." The worst of it seemed to pass. The tension left her face and she slumped back onto the chair, breathing hard. "No hospital. Not now. I need you to hear what I have to say."

"Okay, fine. You win. Say your piece." It was morbid curiosity, that's all. That's what I told myself, anyway. "Then you're out," I added, but the fight had gone out of me. Not much sport in beating up a cancer patient.

"All right." She drew a deep breath. "I want to apologize, Stephen."

"For what?" No way could she get off that easily. "Specifically, for what?"

"For everything. I know I wasn't always a good mother. I made some mistakes that—"

"*Mistakes*! That's your big confession, you made mistakes? You're going to have to do a lot better than that. You threw me out on the street like garbage."

"And I know now that I was wrong."

"Do you know what happens to a sixteen-year-old kid on the streets?"

She seemed to shrink into her woolen coat, like a turtle withdrawing into its shell. "I truly am sorry. I…I never thought…I thought you'd, I don't know, change your mind, and you'd come back, and everything would be okay again."

"It's not something you can just change your mind about. I didn't just make up my mind one morning that this was who I was going to be. This is who I am."

"I realize that now. But back then, I didn't understand."

"You're supposed to be apologizing here, not making excuses. What's the word? *Contrition*, that's it. Didn't the nuns teach you that?"

"I'm not making excuses, just trying to explain. I don't blame you if you're still bitter."

"You know what? I'm really not. I was angry for a long time. Not *bitter*." Such a wimpy, genteel word. "Crazy-assed, fist-through-the-wall angry. But I got over it. I put it so far behind me I hardly ever think of you." It was true. After carrying all that rage around for so many years, clinging to it like it was all I had, I'd finally let it go. Mostly thanks to Eric, the first person in a long, long time to make me believe I was worth something. "And now you come here and drag it all up again, so you can feel better. So, fine." I traced a cross in the air like a priest. "I absolve you. Go now and sin no more."

She didn't move. For a few moments she just sat there, staring at nothing, the ghostly light and shadow from the muted television dancing across her face. "There's more," she said finally. "Something else I need from you."

Should have known. "I can't imagine what I could give you."

Her eyes met mine. "I need your help."

"You've got a lot of nerve. Ask Lisa." I felt shitty saying it. Lisa had carried the whole burden of Mom's illness. "Or Philip. Let the Golden Child help you."

"Philip is too far away. And what I need, I don't think Lisa has the stomach for."

"Okay, I'm curious. No promises," I added quickly, "but I'll hear you out."

"That's fair enough. Stephen, I need you..." She looked down at the talon-like hands twisting the handle of her purse. "I need you to kill me."

"Christ, Mom!" I pushed up from the sofa, banging my knee on the edge of the coffee table. "Ouch! Damn it!"

"Are you okay?"

"No, I'm not okay. Are you out of your freaking mind? Is this some sort of sick Halloween prank?"

"I'm very serious. Serious as cancer, as they say," she added with a faint smile. "And technically, you wouldn't be killing me. Just helping me kill myself."

I stared at her, unable to think of anything to say. The chemo must have fried her brain.

She pulled a second bottle of pills from her bag. "These should do the trick. The others were anti-nausea, otherwise I could throw up and that would be a waste of both our time. And I wouldn't want to mess up your nice rug."

"You mean, right now? You want to do this right now? Here?"

"Did you have other plans for the evening?"

"This is insane."

"I'm dying anyway, you know."

"But Lisa says the chemo—"

"Lisa hasn't faced reality yet. I'm not going to get better."

I sank back onto the sofa, rubbing my bruised knee. "If you're dying anyway, why don't you just wait to die?"

"I'm tired, Stephen. I'm exhausted, I'm in constant pain, and I'm miserable. You probably think I deserve to suffer."

A play for sympathy, or good old Catholic guilt? "Maybe you do."

"Maybe I do. I don't mind paying for my sins. But what I can't stand, I just can't stand the loss of control."

"That sounds more like the Mom I used to know."

"This whole business—the surgeries, the chemotherapy, the *battle*, as they're always calling it—it takes over. Doctors poking and prodding. Like I'm a piece of meat. And for Lisa, it's almost like it's a game she's trying to win."

"That's not fair."

"No, I suppose not. Not a game. Sorry, my mind can get a little clouded sometimes. Things don't always come out the way I want them to. But you know what Lisa's like. Competitive. Hates to lose."

That much was true. She'd been that way since we were little. "She gets that from you."

Mom nodded. "Stubborn Irish, both of us. You too. You're tough."

"I've had to be."

"I know."

Did she know? I wondered. Did she have any idea what I'd been through?

"It's like my body doesn't belong to me anymore. My *life* doesn't belong to me. So I'm taking it back."

"This is a bit extreme, though, don't you think?"

"It's all there is left. My death is all I have left, and damn it, I am going to be in charge." She held out the brown medicine bottle. "Would you mind?"

I stared at it for a moment. Were we really doing this? "Oh, what the hell."

I opened the bottle and handed it back to her.

"Thank you."

"Why here? Why me? Why not in your own home?"

"I thought about that, but I need someone to make sure I don't chicken out. And in the end, I didn't want to die alone. Does that sound pathetic?"

"No, not really." I wouldn't wish that on anyone. Not even her.

"And Lisa would never go along with it. She'll fight to the bitter end to keep me alive. But I thought you would be okay with it. If there's anyone in this world who would appreciate watching me die, it's you."

"Jesus, what a thing to say." I wasn't as ghoulish as that. Was I? "I don't want you to die."

"Really? Well, that's a little disappointing. Not even a little bit? I figured you dreamed about it."

"Well, sure. Every boy dreams. But, you know, I'd always pictured throwing you in front of a freight train or something. Fiery and violent. Not like this."

"This way is better, I think. Less messy."

"How do you even know it will work?" I asked, pointing to the medicine bottle. "How do you know what to take? Or how much?"

She dismissed my concerns with a wave of her hand, diamond rings flashing. "I Googled it, of course. You can find anything on the Internet."

"Huh," was the only reply I could come up with.

"I'm very computer literate these days," she said with a self-satisfied look. "I'm even on Facebook. I'd invite you to friend me, but there'd be no point in that now, would there?"

"No, not if you're really… You're *sure* about this?"

"As sure as anyone can be."

"So, what's going to happen, exactly?" I'd never actually seen anyone die before.

"If these work the way they are supposed to, I'll fall asleep, and then…" She shrugged. "When you're sure I've stopped breathing, wait five minutes, then call 9-1-1. You didn't see me take anything. I simply dozed off while we were visiting and *poof*. Gone."

Sure, I thought. Nothing could go wrong with that plan. Assisted suicide was illegal in New York, I was pretty sure. I could look it up, of course, but that would leave a computer trail.

"Well, you might as well take your coat off and get comfortable," I said. "Looks like you're going to be here for a while."

I helped her out of her coat and hung it in the hall closet next to Eric's raincoat. *Eric*. What was I going to say to him? Could I really do this?

When I came back into the room, she had shaken more than a dozen small, white tablets out onto the table and was already popping one into her mouth. "I'm going to need some more water," she said, draining the last gulp from her glass.

My glass of pinot stood untouched where I'd left it on the end table. I grabbed it and took a long swallow. "How about one of these instead?"

"Oh, the doctors say I'm not supposed to mix—" She cut herself off, giggling. "Sure. Go ahead. One glass isn't going to kill me."

Before I realized what was happening, we were laughing together, loud and long, until my side hurt and I had to sit down. Anyone passing on the street would think we were having a party. When it subsided, I poured her a glass and topped up my own. "Cheers," I said, raising my glass toward her. "Here's to…to what?"

"To absolution?"

"Absolution. Absolutely."

We clinked glasses and she took another pill before sipping her wine. A blissful look smoothed out some of the creases in her face. "Ooh, that's good. It's been a long time."

"You know, I'll be the first to admit I didn't always pay attention. But I'm pretty sure the nuns said this was a sin. You know, what you're doing." What *we're* doing, apparently.

"The nuns." She rolled her eyes. "Dried-up old sticks, what do they know about life? They were wrong about you, weren't they?"

"So you're not afraid of hell?"

"God couldn't be that much of a hard-ass, not for all eternity." Two more pills, chased by a long swig of wine. "If hell exists, it's in this life, not the next."

"You're probably right." I clicked off the TV and turned on the gas flame in the fireplace. I'd wanted a real, wood fire, but Eric insisted on gas. Cleaner and easier, he said, and where would we keep the firewood? "A little atmosphere."

"Nice. Very nice." Another pill. "Cozy."

"Uh, before this gets too far along…"

"Yes?"

"Well, would you mind dying over here?" I pointed to the sofa. "It's just that you're sitting in Eric's favorite chair. I've always hated this sofa, so I won't mind throwing it out. You know…after."

"Of course, dear. No problem."

I helped her get settled and moved her pills closer to her. The wind rattled the window, and she shivered a little. "It's cold out tonight," I said. *Brilliant. Mom's killing herself, and you're blathering about the weather.*

"Lisa will have taken the boys out trick-or-treating. I hope she remembered to dress them warmly."

"I'm sure she did."

"You used to love Halloween, remember?"

"Yeah."

"Loved dressing up. Maybe we should have picked up on that."

"Maybe." I stared into the fire, not looking at her. "This is weird."

"Me killing myself?"

"No. I mean, yeah, that's weird too. But us, I mean, sitting here together. Talking. I never expected this."

"I never expected it either." Another swallow. "But I always hoped."

"Hoped what?" I asked, defensiveness creeping in. "That I'd change?"

"Yes, all right, I hoped you'd change. At first anyway. So sue me. It came as such a blow. You always seemed so normal, then—"

"I *am* normal." Well, more or less. I took a deep breath and another swig of wine to calm myself.

"Yes, yes, okay. You know what I mean. You played football. A linebacker, for heaven's sake. And you dated that cheerleader, what was her name? The Jewish girl?"

"Jenny Stiglitz." I hadn't thought of Jenny in forever, but the name came back instantly. What had happened to her, I wondered. A house in Long Island, probably, with a nice, straight, Jewish husband and two and a half kids.

"That's right. She was sweet."

"You didn't approve of her at the time," I reminded her.

"Well, no. But in retrospect, a Jewish girl seems like small potatoes compared to catching you and Ryan Jenkins in the back seat of your father's BMW." The memory must have disturbed her, because she took two pills in one swallow. "You can hardly blame us for being blindsided by that. And so we...we overreacted."

"There's an understatement." Turning toward her, I saw that her eyelids were starting to droop.

"I kept trying to figure out what I'd done wrong," she said. "That's what they used to say, it's the mother's fault. Coddling, spoiling. But I never coddled you."

"No, you certainly didn't. If you coddled anyone, it was Philip, and he's much too boring to be anything but one hundred percent hetero."

"Be nice." She was going through the pills like salted peanuts. "Now they say that you're born that way, and I wonder, sometimes. You know, I still smoked when I was pregnant with you. I quit before Philip and Lisa. Who knows?"

"I think you can let yourself off the hook, Mom. It's not your fault. It's not a *fault* at all. It just is."

"Later, I just wished you'd come back, whatever you were. But you never did." Her words were starting to slur. How fast was this going to happen? "Stubborn Irish."

"Look who's talking. You could have come looking for me."

She swallowed another one. "I'm here now."

She had me there. Did that make her the better person? I'd need a lot more wine to get my head around that. I refilled both of our glasses and went to the kitchen for another bottle.

"Your father would have taken you back if I'd let him," she said when I came back. "He never forgave me, you know. Do you remember Bettina, from his office?"

"I think so. Kind of vulgar? Peroxide blonde with long red fingernails?" I remember wondering how she typed with those things.

"That's the one. He had an affair with her. Right after you left. Sorry," she waved her hand, warding off any objection I might offer, "after I threw you out. His way of punishing me." She closed her eyes.

The thought of Dad boffing his secretary to avenge me was strangely heartwarming. Didn't know he had it in him. "I'm glad you told me."

It suddenly dawned on me that I *was* glad. I was enjoying this conversation, and it was going to be the last I'd ever have with her. Everything was happening so fast. "Mom," I shouted. "Mom!"

Her eyes snapped open. "What?"

"Are you sure about this? Absolutely sure? If I call an ambulance right now—"

"No, Stephen." She seemed to struggle to focus on me. "You're supposed to be the strong one here, remember? To keep me from backing out. Be brave."

I took another sip of wine to wash down the boulder-sized lump in my throat.

"Come here, beside me." Her hand flapped listlessly against the sofa cushion.

I knelt beside her and took her hand. It felt cold and bony and small in mine.

"You're a good boy, Stephen. I'm proud of you."

"Jesus, Mom." I'd waited twenty-two years to hear those words. Now it seemed there was nothing else we needed to say.

"No, no. Don't cry." With her other hand she reached out and stroked my hair. "My pills, Stephen."

"What?"

"My pills. Not finished yet. Got to do it right. Got to finish. You need to let me go."

I picked up the last two tablets from the coffee table. Mom opened her mouth and, after a moment's hesitation, I placed them on her tongue, like a priest administering communion.

"That's my big, strong boy." She clutched my hand tight as she swallowed. "That's my boy. Now, Stephen."

"Yes, Mom?"

"My funeral. You'll be there, won't you?"

"Wouldn't miss it for the world."

"Closed...closed coffin. Promise me. Don't want...don't want..."

"We don't want those nosy biddies from the country club coming to gawk and gossip about how bad you look."

"That's right. That's right."

"I'll nail the lid shut myself if I have to."

"White...white roses only. Not red or...or yellow. Just white."

"Of course. White roses. Red would be tacky."

"'Zactly. I knew you'd unnerstand. Tell Lisa..."

"Don't worry, Mom. I'll see to everything."

"Good boy. Now, music. Music..."

"How about we start with a rousing chorus of 'Ding, Dong, the Witch is Dead'?"

A faint smile played on her lips. "Nice....That'd be nice."

Timothy Bentler-Jungr has been, at various times, a dishwasher, a bartender, a croupier, an actor/model, an English teacher, an editor, a writer, a diplomatic spouse, and a stay-at-home parent (to name but a few) while living in five countries on three continents.

A single dad, Tim is often found texting story ideas to himself while attending soccer games and school concerts, shopping for groceries, or doing laundry. This is his first published crime short story.

CHRISTMAS

HOPPY HOLIDAYS

by Linda Lombardi

"So how did you get stuck working tomorrow, Hannah?" Margo asked.

I looked up from the miniature snowman I was making out of ice with pieces of fruit frozen inside. Margo stood in front of the bulletin board consulting the weekly schedule.

"I don't mind working holidays," I said. "Especially Christmas."

No need to explain why, not to Margo. I'd been looking forward to my first Christmas at the zoo, because it's the only day we're closed to the public. Yeah, I know that my amazing job only exists because people want to see the animals. Still, a break from the screaming children—and their parents making up information about the animals instead of reading the signs—was the best present I could imagine.

I set a piece of apple peel on top of the fruit-filled snowperson, trying to decide if it looked remotely like a Santa hat. "I don't have any family in the area anyway, so I'm not missing anything."

"I'm only missing the traditional Jewish Chinese food and a movie," Margo said. "And my favorite thing about this job is the excuses it gives me to skip family events."

I nodded. If I had relatives in town, I'd find our work schedule handy that way too. Animals eat every day—at least ours at Small Mammals do, if not those of our lucky friends at Reptiles. And they poop every day. So through rain or storm, dark of night, and weekends, someone has to be here every day, even ones the postman has off. Like Sundays. And Christmas.

"You could bring Chinese to tomorrow's potluck," I said. "Best of both worlds."

Margo smiled and took her dirty food pans to the sink. Shelly walked into the kitchen and took her place in front of the bulletin board.

"You guys, too? I can't believe I have to work Christmas again! Every year I ask for it off, and I never get it. Michael is out to get me. Oh and look—he's the duty curator that day, surprise, surprise. Great way to spend the holiday, with the guy who always ruins it for me."

Margo raised her eyebrows at me, unnoticed by Shelly as she stomped out of the kitchen and up the stairs. "Stomped" in a relative sense. I don't mean it as an insult to say that Shelly is mousy. We small mammal keepers are fans of small rodents. But you'd have to know her well to realize that those footsteps were actually less timid than usual, and how much anger was behind them.

"Is that true?" I asked Margo after the door slammed shut at the top of the stairs.

Margo sighed dramatically. "Indeed. Every year for the last five years we've had to eat the horrible Christmas cookies she makes for the potluck. Whole-wheat, runny frosting that's so sweet your teeth want to jump right out of your mouth, made with some nasty vegetarian shortening, and always burnt on the bottom. And worst of all, they're decorated like little presents with someone's name on each one, so she'll know if you don't eat yours."

"Ugh," I said. "I thought the potluck lunch is supposed to make us feel better about working the holiday, not worse."

"That's why we suck it up and eat them. She obviously puts so much effort into them."

"What can you do? Damn holiday spirit."

"Good will toward incompetent bakers," Margo called after me as I started up the stairs with my little Santa balanced carefully on a pan.

When I got to my keeper area, I climbed into a tamarin exhibit and set the snowman on a ledge, then went out into the hallway to watch the little monkeys run down from the trees and start poking at it. They didn't care that it was holiday-themed, as long as it had mealworms in the crevices. And I didn't care that no one else would see the results of my efforts. The building was peaceful and empty of patrons on a drizzly winter day. Almost like Christmas already, I thought—a moment too soon, because just then a woman and a small boy came down the hall and stopped to stand beside me.

The child pointed into the adjacent exhibit. "What's that?"

"Why don't you ask the nice zookeeper, honey?"

The boy turned and stared at me. I decided to count that as asking, because I was so pleased his mother hadn't just made up an answer.

"It's a tamandua," I said. "It's a kind of anteater."

"Does it bite?" he asked.

Little boys always want to know that. And other people too, especially when they are asking some completely foolish question like whether a golden lion tamarin makes a good pet. The answer is usually that anything with teeth can bite, said in a tone that discourages any ridiculous ideas of having an endangered monkey hanging from their curtains and pooping all over the house. But the tamandua case was a little different.

"Well, an anteater doesn't have teeth," I said, "but see those claws? They're very strong, so she can hang her whole body on them and climb through the trees. She could hurt someone with those claws."

He nodded with satisfaction. Little boys usually prefer if an animal is somewhat perilous. The mother and child moved off and left me happily alone again, gazing dreamily at the tamandua. I thought it was the cutest, most amazing creature I'd ever seen, with its silky, almost shimmery yellow fur and tiny ears and eyes. Watching its incredibly thin, unbelievably fast ant-eating tongue lick gruel off my finger was almost worth cleaning up the horrific and smelly end result. Almost. I had to admit that it seemed to be one of the stupidest animals I'd ever worked with. I guess I shouldn't have been surprised, since it only had room in its skinny little head for a brain the size of a peanut. A shelled peanut, no less. But hey, brains aren't everything, right?

Speaking of which, Michael, our curator, was walking toward me, exactly on time for our appointment. I wasn't standing there to stare at the animals. I don't have time for that sort of thing. There are bales to be hauled and fruit to be chopped and poop to be scooped, a solid eight hours a day. The only reason I was doing nothing for a moment was that I was waiting for Michael, hoping to convince him to let me take the tamandua off exhibit for a while and work on using it for an education animal. It was hand-raised, so it was used to people, and it seemed a waste not to take advantage of that.

Obvious, sure, but maybe not to Michael, who despite being our boss knows nothing about mammals. He's a fish expert, or at least, he used to work with fish, and I assume he must have been an expert in something to be promoted to curator. I mean, I'm sure there is a lot you need to know to work with fish. Water quality. Filtration. Um...water quality? But not behavior or training or most of the things that are second nature to the people he supervises now. And this can be a problem, especially because he loves to climb into exhibits on his own, whether he knows anything about the animals or not. Which he usually doesn't.

"Hannah," Michael said as he strode up to me, sounding a whole lot more cheerful about the encounter than I was.

"Hi." I hopped aside a bit, trying to make it look natural, so I could avoid the trajectory of his breath. A person who goes around all day with poop on her clothes shouldn't throw stones, but Michael has the worst personal hygiene I've ever seen. His breath smells as if he never brushes his teeth—when he smiles you can even see how corroded his gums are.

And his uniform shirts are all stained under the armpits, and that's on a good day when he's wearing one that doesn't have holes there.

"Let's go see what this anteater can do," he said.

My smile was sincere, partly because I was relieved that he was cutting to the chase with no long, smelly conversation first.

"Yeah," I said, and we went around back to climb into the exhibit.

* * * *

"Did you talk to him about its diet?"

My fellow keeper Greg was helping me set up a holding area for the tamandua, after yesterday's successful meeting with Michael.

"No, what about its diet?" I said, peering at the branch I was wiring to the mesh of the cage.

"It eats insects, but we feed it gruel. Why not a more natural diet?"

"I hadn't thought of it, but now that you mention it, if one of my dogs pooped like that I'd definitely be looking for a different food." I stepped back to decide where the next branch should go. "But I should go direct to the nutritionist, given how little Michael knows about mammals. Last weekend Margo copied him when she emailed the commissary to say that our food order was missing the kibble for the fennec fox, and he called and asked, 'What's this *kibble*? Is that a brand name?'" I sighed. "I'm not making that up. I guess he never even had a dog."

Greg smirked. "Still, I prefer his ignorant mode to his inquisitive one."

"Like when he decided to poke around in the South American exhibit and let the saki out," I said. "That was fun."

That had been a couple weeks ago. It had taken an hour out of everyone's day, chasing around the building till we finally netted the stupid primate, who was as freaked out by the experience as everyone else. The problem with being a fish expert is that it doesn't give a guy much practice at getting out of an enclosure without letting any animals run out the door.

"Well, I'd be happy to do some research about the diet," Greg said. "Maybe there's something we could culture ourselves. It would be cheaper that way."

"I'd have thought you took this job to get away from that sort of thing. Not that I'm trying to get rid of you, but if you miss growing fruit flies for frogs, why didn't you apply for that open position in Reptiles?"

There was a silence. "Who says I didn't?" he said after a moment, as if he were trying to make a joke out of it.

"Ah. Well you don't always get what you want around here I guess." Ugh. Obviously he had applied but hadn't gotten it. He was concentrating intently, or pretending to, on the branch he was working on, and I was glad he didn't see how I was blushing.

* * * *

An hour later, as I nibbled on a stuffed mushroom, I considered how weird it was that Reptiles always runs this Christmas Day potluck lunch. They're not usually so sociable with their fellow warm-blooded creatures. Or maybe that's exactly it—they figure this sacrifice takes care of their obligations for the whole year?

It's not just the Reptiles people who are like that, of course. People don't go into working with animals because they get along well with members of their own species. Greg had been totally rude to the new reptile keeper who'd approached him by the lasagna tray a few minutes before, and Shelly had spent the whole party obviously avoiding Michael. So I was relieved when my friend Ray came over and tapped my elbow. Ray will claim he's no more a people person than anyone else at Reptiles, but it was just like him to notice I'd had enough of my fellow humans myself.

"Come see my new dart frogs," he said.

"Sure." I stepped back as Shelly nearly tripped over a chair leg trying to avoid Michael, who was walking by with the half-empty tray of lasagna. "I didn't think you were that interested in frogs."

"Yeah, but I know you're a fan of yellow frogs," he said. "And besides, these are special."

He led me into the back area of the amphibian section, where he proudly pointed to a tank of fat yellow frogs. I peered at them, confused.

"This must be one of those situations where you can only tell them apart by their calls or something?" I said. "They look exactly like the kind you already have." I pointed at the seemingly identical frogs in the adjacent tank.

"Good ID, little mammal person. They are the same species. But note the label on the tank."

"USE GLOVES. Um, exciting. What disease are they carrying?"

"Not a disease. Poison."

"But dart frogs aren't poisonous in captivity. I've heard you tell people that a thousand times. They get the toxins from the insects they eat in the wild, and concentrate it in their skin, and we don't feed them the same insects, blah blah blah."

"Ah, but there's the rub. These are wild caught."

I stared at him for a moment. "So…"

He grinned devilishly. "So this is truly the mighty *Phyllobates terribilis*, often considered the most toxic living animal, with enough poison in its skin to kill a dozen men."

"Ooh."

"As if it mattered. It's still just a frog. You call this perilous? I can handle them with my bare hands if I'm sure there's no broken skin. And as long as I wash my hands before I pick my nose."

I made a face, and, satisfied, he continued, "And that would still only be a problem if my nose was bleeding. The poison has to get directly into the bloodstream. That's why the natives smear the poison on a dart instead of sticking the frog up their prey's nose."

I made another face, just to make him happy. "Yeah, and that would be so much less convenient, too," I said. "Well, even if that's all true, if I want a yellow frog, I'll stick with your Panamanian golden frogs. They're more interesting. These guys are just fat globs who sit there."

"You would just sit there, too, if you could kill anyone who touched you. Well, and then stuck a finger in their bleeding nose." He shook his head sadly at the lame adaptations of frogs that were trying to be poisonous. "At least snakes inject the venom into the bloodstream where it belongs."

"Only you would find it disappointing that an animal's not as dangerous as it's supposed to be. Well, you and every little boy who's ever asked me if something bites," I admitted.

No way that Ray would be the least bit insulted to be put in the same category as small children visiting the zoo, but before he could come up with a witty response to that implication, his radio crackled. "Ray, where's the ice cream scoop?"

"We're not supposed to use the radio for that sort of thing," I said. The radio is only for animal business and emergencies. If you wanted to announce, say, that you'd gotten back from Starbucks with everyone's coffee, you needed to make up a secret code word so the curators wouldn't understand you.

He shrugged. "It's Christmas. Take your time." He waved at the roomful of amphibians.

The door closed behind him, and I crossed the room, squeezing around the big tanks of Japanese giant salamanders. As I watched the much more attractive yellow and black Panamanian golden frogs crawling around—they don't hop, and are technically toads rather than frogs despite their slender shape and smooth skin—I heard the door open again, and the voices of Greg and Michael.

"You have to wash your hands," Greg was saying. "It's not for you, it's for the frogs. They're very delicate."

"Fine, fine," Michael said, as if he were being incredibly indulgent, and I heard the water running in the sink. Michael probably only washes his hands once a day at most. His joke is that he'd spent enough time with wet hands when he worked as an aquarist. Ha-ha. I'm not sure how that's an excuse for the armpit stains, though.

"Okay, here you go. Cup your hand around it and hold firmly. Not too hard—that's good."

Obviously Greg was trying to impress Michael with his amphibian skills so he'd have a better chance of being transferred if there were another opening here. Normally I'd be thinking he had a lot of nerve, taking someone else's animals out of their enclosures. But at least it was better than Michael messing with stuff on his own. He'd have frogs all over the floor in a minute.

"Now you can say you've held one of the world's most deadly animals," Greg said. "No one has to know they're not dangerous in captivity."

The radio crackled and someone announced that it was time for dessert. Oh well, holidays, who cares about the rules?

I waited for the two guys to leave, because dessert is the most important meal of the day, and I didn't want to get into a conversation with Michael and spoil my appetite with his halitosis. He didn't stop at the sink to wash his hands on the way out, of course, and I didn't blame Greg for not saying anything. He'd protected the frogs from Michael's dirty hands. It wasn't his obligation to protect Michael from himself.

As I squeezed around the salamander tank again, I glanced over at the *terribilis* enclosures, and then paused, struck with a familiar, uneasy feeling. I'd learned not to ignore this instinct, because sometimes it meant I'd forgotten to lock something. But most of the time it was nothing, an inconvenient automatic brain-habit born of hundreds of times of double-checking exhibits to make sure they were properly closed.

Still, I'd found it was better to get rid of the feeling by taking some pointless action. It beat having a nagging uneasiness dog me once I was home and couldn't do anything about it.

I walked over to the tanks and made sure they were closed properly. They were fine, of course. This wasn't even my building. Maybe I was getting a little too obsessive. Or maybe I didn't trust anything to be left in order when Michael was around, which was less a sign of incipient mental disability than plain common sense.

And speaking of Michael, I opened the door to leave the frog room, and nearly walked right into him, standing with Greg looking at one of the frog exhibits from the public side.

"Hey! Watch out!" Greg snapped.

"Sorry," I said a bit peevishly. I hadn't bumped into him on purpose. How about not standing right in front of doors? We scowled at each other, and he, Michael, and I walked not exactly together back to the food table. Greg seemed to regain his holiday spirit quickly—the first thing he did was pick up the tray of Shelly's cookies and present it to Michael.

"You've got seniority," he said. "You go first."

Margo was right, the cookies looked absolutely awful. But Shelly was standing there watching, so there was really nothing Michael could do.

"Thanks." He looked at the tray till he found the cookie with his name on it, picked it up, and took a big bite.

"Delicious." He should work on not grimacing when he lied.

As I filled my little plate, he started to lick the nasty drippy frosting off his unwashed hands, and I looked away, not wanting to ruin my enjoyment of the holiday treats, most of which looked a lot more tempting than Shelly's contribution. So I didn't see how it started, and only turned to look when I heard him hit the floor.

Michael's whole body was spasming. Ray ran to him and crouched down, doing some kind of first-aid thing, and someone else ran for the phone.

"Does he have epilepsy or something?" I whispered to Margo.

"Not that I've ever heard," she said.

Everyone who couldn't help moved away a bit, and we stood around awkwardly, holding plates of sweets that we could no longer appropriately eat, but it didn't seem right to just leave and go back to work either…until the ambulance crew burst through the front doors of the building and the party was really over.

* * * *

An hour or so later, Margo and I were working on our afternoon food pans when the phone rang. Margo picked up. "Small Mammals."

After that her side of the conversation was just head-nodding and "Oh! Oh!" and her eyes widening at me.

"What?" I said when she hung up.

"Michael," she said. "He didn't make it."

"What happened?" I asked.

"They think it was some kind of poison," she said. "They won't know what till they do toxicology tests. The police are over at Reptiles."

My eyes grew wide back—and then I looked at the tray of leftover cookies that Shelly had brought back from the party. Margo followed my gaze and looked back at me. Then we both looked toward the keeper lounge off the kitchen, where Shelly was sitting at the computer doing her daily report. Then we both looked back at the tray. To an observer I'm sure it would have seemed funny, how our heads moved in unison, like a couple of meerkats standing on alert.

"No way," I whispered. "It had his name on it. She couldn't be that stupid."

"Ha," Margo whispered back, with forced mirth. "Of course not. The cookies are terrible, but not bad enough to kill someone."

I took my stack of pans and headed up the stairs, thinking, wow, so many things can hurt you at the zoo. Venomous reptiles, lions and tigers, all the tools and dangerous chemicals. Who'd imagine Michael would be done in by a cookie? If it was a cookie, of course. Innocent until proven guilty. Shelly. Wow. It's always the quiet, mousy types, right?

I juggled my stack of food pans so I could unlock the door, and as I stepped into the keeper area, I put my foot down on a paper towel that I recognized. I bent down to pick it up and turned it over. As I suspected, it was the note from the door of my chinchilla exhibit, reminding people not to give him a dust bath because he was being treated for an eye infection. Okay, maybe we ought to write these notes on something more sturdy than a paper towel, but this isn't an office job, it can be really hard to find—

And suddenly something struck me.

That moment I'd had when I thought the frog tanks looked odd. I'd dismissed it as nothing but that automatic habit of re-checking everything on the way out of an area. But now I re-examined the image in my mind and realized what might have changed. The sign, USE GLOVES—had it still been posted on the new frog tank?

I put my pans down and started to walk around the building looking for Greg. I didn't go very fast, because I was feeling sick to my stomach. Maybe Greg and Michael had knocked the sign on the floor as they left. But what if it had already been missing when they got there? Greg was just a little overconfident. What if he was so sure he knew which were the right frogs that he thought he didn't need to look for a sign? What if I'm about to tell him that he might have accidentally killed Michael? Who never washes his hands after handling an animal. And who has terrible bleeding gums, a perfect path to let poison right into his bloodstream when he licked the frosting from a horrible holiday cookie.

I found him outside sweeping leaves out of a drained pool in the lemur exhibit.

"Um, hey, Greg?" I said.

"Yeah?"

"I was just wondering. Um. Remember when you were showing Michael that frog?"

"What frog?"

"The *terribilis*. I was on the other side of the room."

He glanced over at me. "What about it?"

"Um. Ray showed them to me before. There was a sign on the tank warning you to use gloves—"

And suddenly my voice caught in my throat. What if there hadn't been a sign when Greg took out the frog because *I'd* knocked it off when I was walking away? What if it was *my* fault he was dead?

"Yes?" Greg said, a bit impatiently.

"There…there was…" I managed to choke out.

"There was what?" he said, now obviously irritated.

It all came out in a rush now. "There was a sign on the tank that said to use gloves so you knew which frogs were poisonous, wasn't there?"

"Of course," he said.

"Oh." I gasped, relieved. "Oh. Oh, good."

"Why?" he said, clearly peeved at this point.

"Because I think it wasn't there when I left. You must have knocked it off. But I'm sure Ray's put it back by now," I said giddily.

He gave me a final sidelong look as I danced back into the building, relieved that I could go back to suspecting Shelly and her cookies.

* * * *

Holiday potlucks and unexpected deaths, like weekends and bad weather, do nothing to affect the bodily functions of a collection of small mammals. However, they do take up time that you ought to be using for work. There was also all the time I'd wasted trying to move around the building without running into Shelly. I kept telling myself that of course she wouldn't poison a cookie with Michael's name right on it, for Pete's sake, but it didn't help, and I wondered if I looked as obvious as she had when she was trying to avoid Michael at the party. Something she wouldn't have to do anymore, of course.

I figured everyone else was long gone, celebrating whatever dregs were left of the holiday, but I still had to hose the tamandua holding pen one last time before I left. Until Greg came up with a new diet, the end result of the current one needed to be dealt with three times a day. But when I opened the door to my keeper area, I was surprised to discover that I wasn't the only one still here after all. Greg was in the tamandua cage.

I felt a little stab of annoyance. It was one thing if he wanted to mess with other people's frogs, and yeah, he had helped me put the enclosure together, but that didn't give him the right—

"What the…" I sputtered as I ran toward the cage.

I couldn't believe what I was seeing. He was standing on a stool in the holding cage. He needed the stool to reach the crook in the tree branch where the tamandua was curled up—so that he could comfortably hold his pocket tool, open to the biggest, sharpest blade, to the tamandua's soft, furry yellow throat.

"Swear not to tell, or I'll cut her," he said.

"What?" I squealed. "What are you doing? Not to tell what?"

"Don't play stupid. They'll find out what killed Michael when the toxicology comes back. They were supposed to think he was poking around in there on his own."

I stared at Greg with a rush of thoughts spinning round in my head. The warning sign that wasn't on the frogs' tank. The boss who was always messing around in exhibits without asking. The man responsible for refusing to transfer Greg into the job that, I now realized, he had wanted very, very badly. It would have been the perfect crime, if I hadn't stuck around, unseen in a corner, looking at some cute harmless frogs.

"It's just the sort of thing he does, and they'll still believe it, because you won't say anything," Greg hissed. "Because if you say anything, I'll cut her."

"You will not," I said. "Then I'll tell that you did both."

"Your word against mine," he said. "Besides, you won't risk it. You're crazy about this animal."

"You're bluffing," I said with more confidence than I felt. "You'll get fired if you hurt her, and then how are you going to get transferred next time there's a job at Reptiles? Besides, what if I swear now so you'll stop? I can always tell later."

"Oh yeah?" he said. "You won't tell later because you know I can come back in here any time."

He was right. There was nothing I could do to keep him away, to keep the tamandua safe. He had all the same keys that I did to get into the building any time he wanted, when no one was here to see. And there was no way I could prove he'd been with Michael and handed him the wrong frog. It was his word against mine, and his story made so much more sense. Because Michael did do that kind of thing all the time. And who the heck would try to murder someone with a frog?

As my mind raced for a reply, Greg held my gaze and I realized that whatever else he had done wrong, right now he was breaking the most important rule: when you're in a cage, never take your eyes off the animal.

In my peripheral vision, the tamandua started to stir. If it did what I thought it was going to do…

Greg opened his mouth to speak again but it turned into a yelp of pain as the tamandua, oblivious to the danger it was in, reached up for something to hang from and hooked a sharp claw into the soft skin of his forearm.

He flailed about, roaring with pain, nearly dislodging her from the branches. And then he lost his balance on the stool and pitched forward onto the floor.

His head hit the concrete with a sickening thud, and he lay motionless. I stood stunned for a moment myself. What a good thing I had decided not to put mulch on the floor of this cage after all. It was easier to clean this way, and I'd wondered if I was being lazy, but it had turned out to be useful.

Then I came to my senses and ran over to the cage. The tamandua was climbing down toward me on the branch she'd chosen after Greg's arm had pulled away. Luckily it was one that wasn't wired down. I waited for all four claws to be hooked on, then quickly jerked the branch out of place. I dashed out of the cage with the tamandua on the branch, and locked Greg in.

I stood, breathing heavily. "Thanks, peabrain."

The tamandua peered at me nearsightedly. She wasn't thinking about what a clever thing she'd just done. She was looking for a place to climb off of this branch, and my shoulders apparently looked promising.

I heard Greg moan. Quickly I double-checked the lock on the cage door and then started to look around. I knew I needed to call the police. But that would have to wait. First I had to figure out what to do with this anteater.

As a child, Linda Lombardi played with a basket full of plastic animals instead of dolls. Later she left a tenured job at a university to work as a zookeeper and wrote a column about animals for the Associated Press. Linda's revenge for what animals have done to her life is the book *Animals Behaving Badly: Boozing Bees, Cheating Chimps, Dogs with Guns, and Other Beastly True Tales*, and you can read more of the adventures of Hannah and her fellow zookeepers in the mystery *The Sloth's Eye*. Follow her on Twitter at @wombatarama and read more at http://www.lindalombardi.com.

JASMINE

by Debbi Mack

"No one should get away with murder."

Jasmine's words echo in my head as I walk home. I pull my jacket lapels up around my throat to shield it from the wind. I'm tempted to apply more Chapstick to my raw lips, but delving into my purse will slow me down.

The cold is biting. An old year will soon die and a new one will be born, but I have little to look forward to. Not even Christmas, just two days off. Other people will be with their families. I haven't seen mine in years.

Leaning into the wind, the walk from the bus stop seems interminable, even though my apartment building is only a block away.

En route, a tattered wreath on a tavern door catches my eye. It looks as old and used up as I feel. A sign, perhaps? Not likely. More like an excuse. I pause, then head inside for a quick one.

Hustling over and ducking inside as if pursued by ghosts, I shut the door firmly against the elements. A look around tells me I don't belong here. The room is roughly square, illuminated in sickly yellow. Tables and chairs are placed haphazardly, as if tossed about by a careless decorator. A few are occupied. Men drinking alone. Most of them don't notice me. A few spare me a curious glance, only to return to whatever private purgatory they're enduring.

Normally, I don't frequent taverns, but times are far from normal for me lately.

The bar runs along one mirrored wall. Two men sit at it several stools apart. I hesitate.

Oh, who gives a shit? It's a public place.

I walk up to the bar and take a stool between the two men. The bartender, a reed-thin fellow with sandy hair and the suggestion of a goatee, wanders over.

"What can I get you, ma'am?"

I think of movies I've seen and blurt the first words that come to mind.

"Scotch on the rocks, please."

He nods with an approving look. After he pours and sets the drink before me, I take a sip. Goes down smooth as gasoline. Perfect.

"Can I ask you something?" I say to the bartender.

"Sure."

"Do people actually tell bartenders their problems?"

His mouth quirks up in a half-smile. "Sometimes. Dare I ask why?"

I cup the glass with both hands and gaze into it. "A friend of mine is going to prison. She killed someone."

When I look up, the bartender's smile has faded. "I'm sorry. What happened?"

So I tell him.

* * * *

I met Jasmine at a victims' recovery group. To be honest, I knew things about Jasmine before I met her. I work for the police department.

Cops are worse than old ladies and teenage girls when it comes to gossip. And my co-workers gossiped plenty about Jasmine's case. I took a special interest and decided to seek her out and introduce myself. We had a common bond.

Though the name sounded appropriate for a pole dancer, Jasmine turned out to be your basic thirty-something girl-next-door in faded jeans and a long-sleeved peasant blouse. She had light brown hair, doe brown eyes, and a quiet demeanor.

One night I approached her at the coffee table during a bathroom break. She'd just shared her story about being raped and how her attacker was acquitted. I asked her if she was okay.

Her mouth pressed into a thin line, and she blinked rapidly. "It's almost more than I can bear sometimes. Knowing he's out on the streets."

Jasmine didn't want to talk much more about it, so I let it go. However, each time we attended a group session, we'd get together for coffee afterward. She began to open up about her feelings of fear and powerlessness, particularly in light of the acquittal. Week after week she grew angrier. Bordering on rage, really. I kept encouraging her to get it out. I thought I was helping her.

* * * *

"I should have known right there, she was headed for trouble," I tell the bartender, as he pours me another drink.

"Wow. That's…pretty intense. Must be hard for you."

I nod. "To say the least."

He watches me gulp the scotch. "If you don't mind my asking... what happened exactly?"

I suppress a sigh. But then, I'd started this tale. How can I blame him for wanting to know the details? "Well, I made the mistake of buying her a gun. I got it off the street. Easy peasy. I thought it would help her feel better. Feel safer.

"I can see now that was the worst possible thing I could've done." I finish my drink in a single swallow. It burns all the way to my stomach. "She ended up stalking Charles Goodwin, her rapist, and shooting him."

The bartender opens his mouth slightly, then closes it, as his brow furrows. He picks up a rag and wipes the bar. "Wow. How'd they catch her?"

"She turned herself in. Couldn't live with the guilt."

"Well, you can't blame yourself for her actions. She pulled the trigger, not you."

I nod. "Yeah, sure."

He holds up the bottle. "Another?"

I shake my head. "I think I've had enough."

* * * *

When I leave the bar, the wind is still vicious. I cross my arms and buck against the chill. My feet feel like frozen blocks. The two minutes it takes to reach my apartment building seem to last for days, but I finally make it. I stumble toward the elevator. The scotch has gone straight to my head.

I ride the elevator twelve flights up to my floor and get off. After a brief disoriented moment, I find my apartment. I'm starting to warm up from the building's heat, yet my heart remains dead cold. I'd hoped the liquor would help. But it can't change everything that's happened.

Once inside the apartment, I shut the door, but don't bother with the deadbolt or the lights. The city's light pollution provides enough illumination for me to make my way down the hall to my bedroom. Just a double bed, a side table, and a dresser. That's all I need. It's not much, but I despise clutter. I move to the dresser and open the top drawer. The picture is still there, face down. I pick it up and look at it.

Me and Charles Goodwin. My step-brother. Who raped me when I was a teenager and never paid.

Until now.

When the opportunity arose to finally make him pay, I jumped at it. A little push here. A little prodding there. Not that Jasmine really needed it. Helping her get closure in the process was a bonus. At least, that was the plan.

I hadn't counted on how guilty Jasmine would feel. Or that guilt could be catching.

I hadn't counted on caring about Jasmine to the point where her guilt and mine became indistinguishable.

I weave slowly out of the bedroom, down the dark hallway, into the living room. Through a sliding glass door, beyond the balcony, I see a panoramic view of the city's distant hills. Lights like diamonds against a velvet, black sky.

I open the sliding door, and the wind blasts in. A magazine flutters on the coffee table behind me.

I step outside, breathe in the frigid air, and exhale steam that's whipped away in a heartbeat. As I stagger toward the railing, I keep my eyes on the hills and remember Jasmine's last words during our visit at the jail.

"No one should get away with murder."

She was speaking of herself, but I know to whom those words really apply. Grasping the rail, I swing one leg over, then the other. Now, I'm outside the railing, face forward and hanging off by both hands. The railing is freezing and stings my palms. Now, I'm swinging back and forth. The wind whips my hair, which lashes my face. Tears blow away before they can track down my icy cheeks. The ground is far below. I gaze at the hills. Diamonds of light blurring. Moving back and forth. Back and forth.

Finally, I let go. I aim for the horizon and try to fly.

Debbi Mack is the *New York Times* bestselling author of the hardboiled Sam McRae Mystery Series, featuring Maryland lawyer-sleuth Stephanie Ann "Sam" McRae. She has also written and published several short stories and been nominated for a Derringer Award.

Debbi has also written a screenplay that made the quarterfinals cut in the Scriptapalooza contest. Debbi would like to continue writing screenplays and is considering various possible film projects.

A native of Queens, N.Y., Debbi enjoys travel, music, good food, baseball, and the outdoors. Her website is www.debbimack.com.

SAUCE FOR THE GOOSE

by Clyde Linsley

Arthur Gibbs, the celebrated world explorer, considered himself a cosmopolite, a student of the world, and as tolerant an individual as ever lived. So his decision to murder his next-door neighbor was clear evidence of the neighbor's unpleasant nature.

In his varied career, Gibbs had lived on four continents, first as a foreign-service officer with the State Department, then as a highly paid consultant to several multinational corporations. He spoke five languages, four fluently, and held advanced degrees in political science and economics. He could converse easily on almost any subject.

William Lanier, by contrast, was a cretin, intellectually and morally, ignorant of the world around him and indifferent to the events that concerned the world. His interests seemed to be confined to a narrow range of subjects, of which professional sports—notably football—seemed to predominate. Gibbs was not quite sure what Lanier did for a living, but he was certain that his neighbor was a man of little or no value.

If he could have done so, Gibbs simply would have ignored the man, but in the high-rise apartment building where he lived, that was impossible. Lanier was always invading his space, usually at the most inopportune times. Whenever Gibbs invited guests to his apartment, his neighbor would always *happen* to be in the hall to greet them, busily engaged in some important but obscure activity and always (it seemed to Gibbs) fishing for an introduction or an invitation. It was distressing; the man was always on his best behavior, so guests would wonder why he was *not* invited. Weren't they neighbors, after all? His friends, he felt, were beginning to wonder about his behavior. But it would be even worse if he included Lanier, so that his friends would learn the man's true nature and associate him with his loutish neighbor.

Gibbs had considered his alternatives. He could move, of course, but it would be difficult—perhaps impossible—to find comparable lodgings in the crowded city. For the same reason, it would be difficult to make conditions so uncomfortable that Lanier would elect to move away.

Facing such dismal prospects, Gibbs decided to make one last attempt to accommodate his neighbor's desire to be sociable in a way that would not destroy his own reputation. A half-hearted effort, to be sure, but as sincere as he could make it. Because the holiday season was approaching, he invited Lanier to a Christmas dinner.

Lanier quickly accepted the invitation. Gibbs determined to make the best impression possible, and he was certain that he could do so. He prided himself on his culinary skills. A Christmas goose, he decided, was the perfect offering—a traditional holiday feast, but one not normally offered in an era of "quick and easy."

He took great care to purchase the perfect goose, neither too fat nor too lean, and he devoted hours to its preparation. While the bird roasted, he prepared an accompanying compote of apples and sage. The result, he concluded proudly, was superb. The best he had ever done.

The dinner, alas, was disastrous.

Lanier was late in arriving—two hours late. He apologized profusely, explaining that he had been engrossed in "the game."

"Game?" Gibbs asked. "What game?"

"Why, the Redskins, of course," Lanier said. "They're playing the Cowboys this week, and—don't tell me you haven't been watching it."

"I don't have television," Gibbs said. "Never saw the need."

Lanier's jaw dropped. "No TV? How do you keep up with things?"

"I get two daily newspapers," Gibbs said. "Three, actually, if you include the *Wall Street Journal*, which I don't because it's such a specialized publication."

Lanier stared at Gibbs in disbelief.

"And I have radio, of course," Gibbs added.

"And you follow the news on the radio?"

"Well, no. Opera, mostly. There was a performance of *Les Troyens* just last night. Quite enjoyable."

Lanier shook his head in disgust. "Whatever," he said.

The evening went downhill from there. Conversation was virtually non-existent. Lanier ate almost nothing, saying that he disliked goose.

He did seem to enjoy the compote of apples and sage. In fact, he helped himself to several servings, which he consumed, although still silently, with obvious relish. And when the evening was over, he turned to Gibbs and shamefacedly asked if he could have the recipe.

Gibbs was taken aback. He would not have been surprised at a request for the goose recipe; he considered it one of his specialties. The apple compote, however, had been an afterthought, and he had not followed a recipe. It had been an experiment from start to finish, and he did not remember all that he had done to make it.

But an idea came to him suddenly. If he *could* duplicate the dish, or make something similar to it, and introduce one subtle and toxic addition, it would work out nicely, and remove the man from his life at the same time. As long as Lanier did not detect the differences between the original dish and its successor—and Gibbs was certain he would not—Lanier would go to his death unaware that he had been poisoned. It would be, in a sense, the perfect murder.

"I'm sorry," he told Lanier, sounding as sincere as he could. "The recipe was given to me by an old friend, who asked that I never divulge the details to another soul."

"Oh, well," the crestfallen Lanier said. "In that case, I understand. I wouldn't want you to betray a friendship."

"But what I *could* do," Gibbs continued, "is make *another* serving of my sauce just for you. That wouldn't be breaking my promise to my friend."

"You'd do that for me?" Lanier said.

"Of course," Gibbs said. "I'd be happy to do so. It'll take a few days, but…"

"I don't care," Lanier said hastily. "Take as long as you need. I'm going to enjoy that stuff."

"I'm certain of that," Gibbs said with a smile. He began immediately to put his plan in motion.

Gibbs had an ace in the hole: an acquaintance in one of the government intelligence agencies had told him of a special poison that was odorless and tasteless and would be almost undetectable unless one were looking for it specifically. He called it ricin.

"You have to be very careful when you make it," the acquaintance had told him. "But ricin isn't particularly difficult to make. You make it from castor beans, which you can probably get at a hardware store or a garden center, and you can find the recipe on the internet."

A quick search yielded the information he sought, and Gibbs set to work immediately. The process took several days, and Gibbs had to be careful to avoid accidental exposure to the poison, which was quite virulent.

When the ricin was ready, Gibbs prepared the compote, mixed in the ricin—carefully avoiding spillage—and delivered the dish to Lanier, who received it gratefully.

"Great," Lanier said. "Hey, I owe you. Is there anything I can do for you?"

Yes, there is, Gibbs thought but did not say. *And you shall soon provide it.*

“There’s really nothing I need,” he said, instead. “I was happy to be of assistance.”

How long would it take for the ricin to kill his neighbor? After carefully disposing of the potentially contaminated garments he’d worn and scrubbing his entire kitchen from ceiling to floor, several times, Gibbs sat down and consulted his notes. It might take a few weeks, or a few days, depending on how much of the compote Lanier consumed before it took effect. The first signs might be much like the symptoms of a cold or influenza. They would grow rapidly more severe until, one day, he would simply succumb.

But Lanier did *not* succumb. Days passed without incident. Gibbs had not expected Lanier to announce that he was dying, but his appearance and demeanor remained unchanged.

Gibbs found himself lying in his bed, wide awake, long hours into the night, listening for the siren of a fire-and-rescue truck, or the sound of heavy boots in the hallway as hastily summoned firemen and paramedics rushed up the stairs to Lanier’s apartment. Gibbs imagined the glee he would feel when he heard a medical professional declare his neighbor to be, officially, dead.

No such announcement was issued, and Lanier remained very much alive. Each morning, Gibbs would enter the hallway and find his neighbor also standing there. Each morning, Lanier would smile at Gibbs as if greeting a long-lost friend. He would make small talk in the elevator, as if nothing untoward had happened. Gibbs found himself wondering whether he had actually attempted to poison the man.

Perhaps he had dreamt it all? But a quick check of his storage unit revealed the tiny, tightly capped bottle of ricin he’d hidden there, still waiting for him to devise a safe method of disposal.

He could not imagine what had gone wrong with his plan. He knew only that the attempt to murder his neighbor had been unsuccessful. But he knew, also, that he would never have the courage for another attempt. If the deed itself was not sufficiently off-putting, the long ordeal of fruitless waiting was quite sufficient.

Gibbs made his peace with the situation. Perhaps it was time to begin the search for a new place to live—an apartment far away from his present lodgings. He made up his mind to begin the search the following day.

In the morning he made calls to several rental agents in town and made appointments to look at some apartments that had only recently become available. As he slipped into his overcoat, his doorbell rang.

“Good morning,” Lanier said.

“Mr. Lanier!”

"Oh, I think our friendship's gone beyond Mr. Lanier and Mr. Gibbs. Don't you think so, Arthur?"

"I suppose so," Gibbs said. He waited for Lanier to state his business.

"May I come in?" Lanier said.

"I was just going out," Gibbs said. "Is this something that could wait?"

Lanier frowned and shook his head. "Don't think so," he said. "I need your opinion on something important. Important and urgent."

Puzzled, Gibbs moved aside so Lanier could enter. His neighbor went into the living room and quickly took a seat on the sofa. He opened the small paper bag he carried, removing a plastic container with a lid, which he placed on the table before him.

Gibbs waited impatiently for Lanier to continue, but his neighbor seemed to have lost his sense of urgency. He sat quietly, his eyes roaming around the room for what seemed an eternity. Gibbs was about to ask his business when Lanier finally spoke up.

"Nice place," he said. "I really like what you've done with it. These newer buildings don't have much character, but I like the way you've made this space your own."

"Thank you." Gibbs waited, but Lanier seemed in no hurry to proceed to business. After a long moment, Gibbs felt the need to move the discussion forward.

"So what can I do for you, Mr.—"

"Jim, please," Lanier said. "Or James, if you insist on being formal. I'd prefer Jim. Just Jim."

"All right, Just Jim," Gibbs said. "What can I do for you?"

"I was quite impressed with the sauce you whipped up for Christmas dinner," Lanier said. "Since I'm having a few friends over for dinner next week, I decided to try making something like it. Have I managed to capture the flavor of yours?"

The "sauce," Gibbs noted, was in a plastic container like those that eager salesmen hawked door-to-door. Gibbs would never have put anything in such a tacky, middlebrow container. Wrinkling his nose, he took the container from Lanier and removed the lid. He sniffed it judiciously.

"It certainly has the right aroma," Gibbs said. "Of course, that's not a definitive judgment. I'd have to taste it to be sure."

"By all means," Lanier said with enthusiasm. "Let me get you a spoon. I really want your opinion."

He sprang from his seat and hurried to Gibbs's kitchen, returning quickly with the utensil.

"Please," he said as he handed Gibbs the spoon. "Let me have it straight. I can take it."

Gibbs took the spoon and dipped into the compote. The flavor that greeted him was as familiar as an old friend. His face registered his recognition. He quickly dipped his spoon back in and savored another, larger portion.

"Does that smile mean that I have succeeded?" Lanier asked.

"You have, indeed." Gibbs took another, larger spoonful. "If I didn't know better, I'd guess that you had duplicated my achievement perfectly."

"Well, not quite," Lanier said.

"I beg your pardon?" Gibbs asked, after swallowing his third spoonful of the compote.

"I didn't *duplicate* it," Lanier said. "I merely transferred it from your container to one of mine. You're correct that this is quite like your own creation. That's because it *is* your creation."

Gibbs's spoon froze halfway to his mouth.

"But why—" he exclaimed.

"Why? Did you think your sudden gesture of friendship wouldn't seem suspicious, after years of getting the cold shoulder? You were pathetically obvious. I racked my brain, trying to figure out what you were up to. And I realized you were faking it—you had some sort of dirty trick up your sleeve."

"But surely you didn't think I would try to *harm* you," Gibbs said, realizing as the words left his mouth just how lame his protest sounded.

"Well, I didn't know, did I? How *could* I know? But I thought it was possible. I needed to find out. And from the sick look on your face, I'm guessing my suspicions were on the money."

"Oh, God," Gibbs said.

"It's no use blaming God," Lanier said. "You can get an explanation from God face to face pretty soon. And I'm sure he'll be interested in *your* explanation, as well."

"And how will *you* explain *yourself*?" Gibbs said heatedly. "Do you think God will ignore murder?"

"I don't think of it as *me* committing murder," Lanier said. "I think of it as *you* committing suicide."

After Lanier left, Gibbs thought about his dilemma. Perhaps he hadn't added sufficient quantities of ricin to the compote. But he knew that he had done everything correctly.

He could go to the emergency room. But would they even know what ricin was? And it would likely be days or weeks, even, before he could find a specialized physician capable of applying an appropriate antidote, if one existed. Surely there was something—something exploratory or experimental perhaps—that could alter his fate and improve his prognosis.

But in order to seek a cure, he realized, he would be forced to explain his circumstances: how he had attempted to murder his neighbor, and how it had all gone wrong. Could he live with that knowledge? More to the point, could others—people he admired and respected—admire and respect *him* if they knew what he had done? Would he be able to face them if they knew?

On the other hand, if he died, there would be a funeral, and perhaps a memorial service, at which various people would deliver eulogies. That could only enhance his reputation. He could also specify in his will that Lanier be invited to speak on that occasion. Would Lanier be tempted to explain the circumstances of Gibbs's death, including Gibbs's failed homicide attempt? Perhaps, but Gibbs thought such an attempt would backfire.

What sort of man, after all, would speak ill of the deceased? And at the decedent's own memorial?

He realized that he was developing a cough and a sore throat. He would probably feel even worse in the morning. Perhaps it would be best simply to let nature take its course and leave his reputation intact.

He would die, of course, but he would have protected his reputation, and a man's reputation was—after all—his most valuable possession. He was surprised to find that the thought was rather comforting.

Clyde Linsley is a refugee from journalism who now writes historical fiction because he likes history. His most recent novels featured Yankee lawyer Josiah Beede. "Sauce for the Goose" is more contemporary, however. Linsley lives in the Virginia suburbs of Washington, D.C.

A CHRISTMAS TRIFLE

by Donna Andrews

I spent almost a minute beating the alarm clock before realizing the ringing came from the phone.

"Yeah," I said, hoping I was holding the receiver right side up.

"Meg, this is an emergency! How soon can you get here?"

"Who is this, and where is 'here?'"

Okay, so I wouldn't win any charm contests at six a.m. I'm not used to being awake at that hour, much less coping with emergencies.

"It's Aunt Rose, and I need you right away! Someone has tried to poison Stanley!"

I should have known. These days my whole family seemed to think I was some kind of female Sherlock Holmes.

"Have you called the police?" I asked, sitting up and shoving the hair out of my eyes.

"They won't do anything," Aunt Rose said. "We need you."

"All right. I'll get there as soon as I can."

I hung up the phone and sighed. I already had plans for the day, and Aunt Rose wasn't part of them.

"What's going on?" The main object of my now-postponed Friday plans stuck his head out from under the comforter, blinking sleepily.

"Aunt Rose was on the phone," I said. "Apparently Uncle Stanley is visiting, and she thinks someone has tried to poison him."

"I remember Uncle Stanley," Michael said, yawning. "The judge. The one who threw us that nice party when we got back from our honeymoon. I don't remember meeting an Aunt Rose."

"Well, now's your chance. Get dressed," I said, grabbing a sweater from the floor. "I promised her I'd go over right away."

Since Aunt Rose lived in Richmond, an hour's drive away even without Friday rush hour traffic, 'right away' took longer than I liked.

"Don't worry," Michael said, for the hundredth time, as he navigated the quiet streets of Aunt Rose's neighborhood nearly two hours later. "I'm sure Uncle Stanley will be all right. We'll figure out what's wrong."

"I hope so," I said. "There, that's her house."

"Which one?"

"End of the block." I pointed. "With the snowman in the yard."

Michael gave me an odd look.

Normally there's nothing odd about having a snowman in your yard, except that it was only mid-October, and it hadn't snowed yet. For that matter, the last two winters had been exceptionally mild, and it had been a good thirty months since we'd had enough snow to make a snowball, much less the enormous snowman gracing Aunt Rose's lawn.

"It's not real snow," I said.

"I suspected as much."

"Part of her holiday decorations."

"Really."

He was getting that look again. That look that made me wonder if Aunt Rose would be the last straw; if she would be the crazy relative who finally made him sit up and say, "Meg's whole family is absolutely bonkers! What have I let myself in for? Is it too late to get an annulment?"

"She really goes all out, doesn't she?" was what he eventually said.

Apart from the snowman, we saw a life-sized wooden nativity scene one of the cousins had carved and painted, with more enthusiasm than skill. A bright red sleigh, with its eight reindeer, perched on the roof. And, of course, sticking out of the chimney, a fairly realistic set of legs with polished black boots attached as if Santa had taken a nosedive down the chimney.

More reindeer grazed on the lawn, including one with a red lightbulb blinking where his nose ought to be. Another enterprising cousin had transformed several dozen garden gnomes into elves to create a detailed Santa's workshop tableau.

Fir garlands and red bows decked the picket fence. A wreath the size of a truck tire graced the front door. Electric candles stood on the inside windowsills with glass ornaments hanging above them. Aunt Rose hadn't turned on the lights, but I could tell that every tree in the yard was wired from root to crown, and the eaves were dripping with those new icicle-style lights.

"Wait till you see the inside," I said.

Michael smiled. He thought I was kidding. I watched his jaw drop when the door swung open.

The hall alone contained enough evergreen garlands to strip a twenty-foot spruce—had they not been made of plastic—several miles of velvet ribbon, and a small artificial Christmas tree. An elaborate concoction of bells, blinking lights, and mistletoe dangled from the chandelier, and more bells and mistletoe graced each of the three doorways leading out of the hall. The smell of evergreen alone would have been pretty strong—she must have used several cans of holiday-scented air freshener—but it was almost lost in the overpowering reek of cinnamon and spices wafting from the kitchen. I could hear Bing Crosby crooning "White Christmas" somewhere in the background.

Normally, Aunt Rose would have given us an hour-long house tour so we could admire the decorations. Not this time. She barely let us get our coats off before leading us to the problem.

"Thank God you're here!" she exclaimed. "I've been worried sick. He's right in here under the Christmas tree. The big one in the living room," she added, seeing Michael glance at the small tree behind her.

"Under the Christmas tree?" I glanced over at it. "What the—?"

It wasn't Uncle Stanley lying under the Christmas tree but a large, gray tabby. The several hundred elaborately wrapped fake presents Aunt Rose usually spread out under the tree had been shoved aside to make a space on the red velvet tree skirt for the cat.

"This is Stanley?" I asked.

"Yes," she whispered. "I'm cat-sitting for my neighbor. She's on a three-month around-the-world cruise. She'll never forgive me if anything happens to him."

I frowned at Stanley. An open can of cat food lay by his head—an expensive brand, if the small size of the can was anything to go by. He was ignoring it. He was also ignoring the fur mouse, the catnip ball, and the scattering of cat treats lying around him.

"Hello, Stanley," I said.

He raised his head slightly, inspected me briefly, then closed his eyes and slumped back onto the velvet.

"He just lies there like that," Aunt Rose whispered.

"Have you—?" I began.

"Shh!" Aunt Rose said. "Let's go out in the kitchen where we won't disturb him."

We tiptoed into the kitchen. The Christmas elves had struck here, too. Another tree occupied most of the space on the table. Unlike the one in the living room, which was an all-purpose ten-foot artificial tree covered with an assortment of ornaments, this was a theme tree—all the ornaments were edible. My stomach rumbled to remind me that I'd skipped breakfast.

I parked Aunt Rose in a chair and sat beside her. I had to crane my neck slightly to see her past the lower branches of the tree.

"Have you taken him to the vet?" I asked.

"Three times now. He's had every test in the book, all negative. We've changed brands on his cat food and his kitty litter. Nothing helps.

The vet thinks he's being poisoned. Repeatedly. Tells me to keep him inside, put away any rat poison. Well I don't let him go outside, and I wouldn't put down poison for anything, not even roaches, if I had them, which I assure you I do not, any more than I have rats. The idea! And I haven't let anyone but you in for two days now!"

"Calm down," I said, patting her shoulder. "We'll figure it out. How about some tea? That'll make you feel better."

"I'll make it," Michael said, walking over to the stove and peering into a pot that was steaming on the back burner. "Or better yet, how about some of this hot cider Aunt Rose has all ready?"

"Sounds good," I said.

"Hot cider?" Aunt Rose seemed puzzled.

Michael held out two steaming cups. "I'll make tea if you prefer."

"No, I'll take cider," I said, taking a cup from his hand and inhaling the rich cinnamon-apple smell.

"No! Don't drink that!" Aunt Rose said, springing to her feet. She grabbed my arm, spilling some of the cider.

"Ouch!" I said. "Why not? Are you saving it for something?"

"It's not cider; it's a stovetop sachet," she said, taking the cups and bustling over to the stove. "You boil it to make the house smell good; you're not supposed to drink it. There's a warning label on the package: not for human consumption."

"Do you suppose Stanley got into the ersatz cider?" Michael asked, as Aunt Rose poured the fragrant liquid back into the pot.

"No," I said. "But I bet I know what he has gotten into."

I marched back into the living room, with Michael and Aunt Rose trailing in my wake. "Okay, half of this stuff has got to go," I said.

"What do you mean?" Aunt Rose asked.

"Poinsettias: poisonous, according to Dad," I said, pointing to a dozen flower pots massed on the coffee table. "They probably wouldn't kill Stanley—that's a myth. But they could give him a serious upset tummy. Has he been sick to his stomach?"

"Oh, yes," Aunt Rose said. "Repeatedly. All over the presents."

Did the poinsettias show feline tooth marks on their lower petals? Hard to tell. Even if they didn't, there were plenty more elsewhere in the house—I could see several dozen white ones through the dining room arch.

"Mistletoe: also poisonous," I said, pointing to the mantle. "To people, at least; can cause convulsions in children when they eat it. The holly berries: toxic. Also those beautiful white lilies. Deadly to cats. And I'm not quite sure, but I think that red cyclamen and all those beautiful red amaryllises are poisonous, too."

"Your dad's the expert on poisonous plants," Michael said. "Maybe we should call him."

"He'd only say the same thing," I said. "That we should start getting rid of all these dangerous plants."

"All my Christmas plants!" Aunt Rose wailed. She was glaring at Stanley.

"Just until your neighbor reclaims Stanley," I said.

"That's not till after New Year's," Aunt Rose said.

"We'll stow them upstairs in your guest rooms for the time being."

It took over an hour, but we emptied the downstairs of toxic plants. Stanley lay watching us with his ears laid back. About the time we dragged the last poinsettia upstairs, he condescended to stagger to his feet and nibble a bit of cat food.

"See," Michael said. "He's better already."

Tired of being ignored was my diagnosis. Our efforts might prevent a recurrence of the problem, but they couldn't have cured Stanley that fast. Clearly, Stanley was the feline equivalent of a drama queen. Or maybe he shared my impatience with Aunt Rose's over-the-top observance of Christmas.

"Now keep your eyes open, and make sure he stays out of the guest rooms," I said aloud as Michael and I were putting on our coats.

"Ten more weeks," Aunt Rose said, looking around. "A whole holiday season. My poor house."

The house looked worlds better, if you asked me. Less like an overstocked Christmas boutique. I decided it wouldn't be tactful to say so.

"Cheer up," Michael said. "This gives you a great excuse not to cat-sit in the future. Or dog-sit, for that matter."

"Hmmm…"Aunt Rose said, looking over her shoulder at Stanley, who was eyeing her red velvet couch as if to assess its suitability as a scratching post. "That's true. And thank you for coming, Meg. I knew you'd crack the case."

"No problem. Though Dad could have done the same thing. Or your vet, if he did house calls."

Aunt Rose stood on her doorstep, waving to us as we got into the car.

"You know," I said as I started the engine. "There was an easier solution. I just couldn't bring myself to suggest it."

"Nothing that would hurt Stanley, I hope."

"Of course not! We could have volunteered to keep Stanley," I said. "Maybe we still should. We both like cats. I wouldn't mind if we got one someday. Aunt Rose would feel so much better if she could put her plants back. And there's nothing in our miserable little basement apartment that would poison poor Stanley."

"Not yet," Michael said. "But there will be."

He reached behind the seat and pulled out a paper bag.

"I swiped a good deal of the mistletoe while we were undecorating," he said, tucking a sprig of it behind my ear. "I'm sure we can find something interesting to do with it for the rest of the weekend."

I glanced in the rear-view mirror. Aunt Rose stood in her doorway, still waving at us. Stanley was sitting in one of the windows, eyeing the fragile-looking glass ornament dangling over his head. I saw him draw back his paw and bat the ornament off its mooring. I probably only imagined hearing the delicate tinkle of breaking glass, but I definitely wasn't imagining Aunt Rose's shriek of horror.

"Yes," I said. "Stanley will definitely have more fun with Aunt Rose."

Donna Andrews is the author of twenty-two published mysteries. *The Good, the Bad, and the Emus* (Minotaur, July 2014) is the seventeenth book in the Meg Langslow series, and *The Nightingale Before Christmas* (Minotaur, October 2014) is the eighteenth. She has been a coordinating editor of the Chesapeake Crimes anthology series since the first volume. You can find her at http://www.donnaandrews.com, at the Femmes Fatales blog (http://femmesfatales.typepad.com), on Facebook (https://www.facebook.com/DonnaAndrewsBooks), on Twitter (@DonnaAndrews13), and at her computer, working on the next book.

ABOUT THE EDITORIAL PANEL AND COORDINATING EDITORS

Christina Freeburn served in the JAG Corps of the U.S. Army and also worked as a paralegal and librarian. The Faith Hunter Scrap This Mystery series brings together her love of mysteries, scrapbooking, and West Virginia. Recently, she completed writing a five-part inspirational romantic suspense series, New Beginnings, featuring skip-tracers who relocate women needing a new life.

When not writing or reading, she can be found in her scrapbook room or at a scrapbooking crop. She lives in West Virginia with her husband, children, a dog, and a cat rarely seen except by those who are afraid of or allergic to felines.

John Gilstrap is the *New York Times* bestselling author of *End Game*, *High Treason*, *Damage Control*, *Threat Warning, Hostage Zero*, *No Mercy*, *Nathan's Run*, *At All Costs*, *Even Steven*, *Scott Free*, and *Six Minutes to Freedom*. In addition, John has written four screenplays for Hollywood, adapting the works of Nelson DeMille, Norman McLean, and Thomas Harris. Outside of his writing life, John is a renowned safety expert with extensive knowledge of explosives, hazardous materials, and fire behavior.

Alan Orloff is the author of *Diamonds for the Dead* (an Agatha Award finalist for Best First Novel) and the Last Laff Mystery series (*Killer Routine and Deadly Campaign*). Writing as Zak Allen, he's published three e-book originals: *First Time Killer*, *Ride-Along*, and *The Taste*. Alan is treasurer of the Mid-Atlantic Mystery Writers of America chapter, is a member of Sisters in Crime and International Thriller Writers, and leads workshops at The Writer's Center in Bethesda, Maryland. For more info, visit www.alanorloff.com.

Marcia Talley is the author of *Tomorrow's Vengeance* and twelve previous novels featuring Maryland sleuth Hannah Ives. A winner of the Malice Domestic Grant and an Agatha Award nominee for Best First Novel, Marcia won an Agatha and an Anthony Award for her short story

"Too Many Cooks" and an Agatha Award for her short story "Driven to Distraction." She is editor of two mystery collaborations, and her short stories have appeared in more than a dozen anthologies. She divides her time between Annapolis, Maryland, and sailing with her husband aboard Troubadour in the Bahamas. www.marciatalley.com

Bios for **Donna Andrews** and **Barb Goffman** appear with their stories.

Made in the USA
San Bernardino, CA
26 September 2014